P9-DCB-915

"This is twice in two days that you've been there when I needed a friend."

The last word came out a little stiff. It was silly to think there could ever be more between them even if an out-of-touch piece of her heart wanted more.

He lifted his chin, like he was doing what any decent man would.

Little did he know there'd been a shortage of decent men in Kelly's life.

"Thank you for making so many sacrifices in order to help me." She held tight to his hand. "I don't know where I'd be right now if it wasn't for you, but I'm fairly sure it wouldn't be anywhere I'd want to be. And I'm also pretty sure that I seem like a train wreck to you, but I'm actually pretty normal."

More moisture gathered in her eyes.

Will thumbed away a rogue tear.

And then he leaned in and pressed a kiss to her lips. "I've never been especially fond of normal."

RANSOM AT CHRISTMAS

USA TODAY Bestselling Author

BARB HAN

If you purchased this book without a cover you should be aware that this book is stolen property. It was reported as "unsold and destroyed" to the publisher, and neither the author nor the publisher has received any payment for this "stripped book."

All my love to Brandon, Jacob and Tori,
my favorite people in the world.

To Babe, my hero, for being my great love and
my place to call home.

Recycling programs for this product may not exist in your area.

ISBN-13: 978-1-335-60470-5

Ransom at Christmas

Copyright © 2019 by Barb Han

All rights reserved. Except for use in any review, the reproduction or utilization of this work in whole or in part in any form by any electronic, mechanical or other means, now known or hereafter invented, including xerography, photocopying and recording, or in any information storage or retrieval system, is forbidden without the written permission of the publisher, Harlequin Enterprises Limited, 22 Adelaide St. West, 40th Floor, Toronto, Ontario M5H 4E3, Canada.

This is a work of fiction. Names, characters, places and incidents are either the product of the author's imagination or are used fictitiously, and any resemblance to actual persons, living or dead, business establishments, events or locales is entirely coincidental.

This edition published by arrangement with Harlequin Books S.A.

For questions and comments about the quality of this book, please contact us at CustomerService@Harlequin.com.

® and TM are trademarks of Harlequin Enterprises Limited or its corporate affiliates. Trademarks indicated with ® are registered in the United States Patent and Trademark Office, the Canadian Intellectual Property Office and in other countries.

Printed in U.S.A.

USA TODAY bestselling author **Barb Han** lives in north Texas with her very own hero-worthy husband, three beautiful children, a spunky golden retriever/standard poodle mix and too many books in her to-read pile. In her downtime, she plays video games and spends much of her time on or around a basketball court. She loves interacting with readers and is grateful for their support. You can reach her at barbhan.com.

Books by Barb Han

Harlequin Intrigue

Rushing Creek Crime Spree

Cornered at Christmas
Ransom at Christmas

Crisis: Cattle Barge

Sudden Setup
Endangered Heiress
Texas Grit
Kidnapped at Christmas
Murder and Mistletoe
Bulletproof Christmas

Cattlemen Crime Club

Stockyard Snatching
Delivering Justice
One Tough Texan
Texas-Sized Trouble
Texas Witness
Texas Showdown

Harlequin Intrigue Noir

Atomic Beauty

Visit the Author Profile page at Harlequin.com.

CAST OF CHARACTERS

Kelly Morgan—She can't explain why she's on the run or has blood on the white wedding dress she's wearing.

Will Kent—This serious Kent brother is focused on finding the man responsible for butchering the family's livestock. The last thing he needs or wants is a distraction.

Christina Foxwood—Is Kelly's cousin an innocent victim, or does she have secrets?

Bobby Flynn—What does this prison inmate know about the accident that took the lives of Kelly's father and brother?

Zach McWilliams—A fine lawman, but are his suspicions misguided in this case?

Mr. Morgan—Is this man's past coming back to haunt his daughter?

Fletcher Hardaway—Does this successful Fort Worth entrepreneur have something to hide?

Chapter One

Torpedoing through trees at breakneck speed, Kelly Morgan drew a frustrating blank as she glanced down at the intricately detailed bodice of the white dress she wore. Branches slapped at her face and torso, catching the puffy layers of the full-length dress. She pushed ahead, anyway, because a voice in the back of her mind rang out, loud and clear.

It shouted, *Run!*

Trying to recall any details from the past few hours, let alone days, cramped her brain. All she remembered clearly was that there'd been a man in a tuxedo trying to force some kind of clear liquid down her throat.

Other than that, Kelly was clueless as to what she was doing in a white dress and her dress cowgirl boots barreling through the woods on a random ranch.

A cold front had moved in and she was shivering in her formal attire. Instinct told her to follow the creek.

As she fought her way through the underbrush,

a vine caught the toe of her right boot. Her ankle twisted, shooting pain up her leg and causing her to stumble forward a few steps as she tried to regain balance.

Those couple of steps couldn't stabilize her.

Momentum shot her forward onto all fours.

Thankfully, she missed banging her head on a mesquite tree by scarcely two inches. Her knees weren't so lucky. They scraped against thorny branches. Rocks dug into her palms as she landed on the hard, unforgiving earth.

It was probably adrenaline that stopped her from feeling the pain of her knees being jabbed by rough edges and her hands being cut by sharp rocks.

Or whatever was in that glass of water the tall, bulky tuxedo-wearing male figure had forced down her throat.

"Tux" seemed familiar but she couldn't pull out why. And the drink he'd tried to shove down her throat? Kelly had instantly figured out that it was laced with something. The second that tangy liquid had touched her tongue, she realized how much trouble she was in. The tacky metallic taste must be what it would have been like to lick a glue stick that had been dipped in vinegar.

Of course, she'd spewed out as much of the liquid as she could, but then the dark male figure—why couldn't she remember who he was or the details of his face?—had pushed her a few steps backward until her back was flat against the wall. He'd pressed his body against hers, pinning her. He'd been so close, mere inches from her face, and yet she couldn't recollect the details of his face. She'd struggled for control of the glass before he forced the liquid into her mouth.

All she recalled next was the gross metallic taste and the overwhelming feeling she wanted—no, needed!—to vomit. The cool liquid had made gurgling noises in her throat as he forced back her head. The room had spun as a dark cloud wrapped around her, squeezing, suffocating her.

Instinct told her to fight back and get out of the bride's room of the small wedding chapel. But why she'd been there in the first place was still fuzzy.

The memory caused a rocket of panic to shoot through her and her brain to hurt. She pushed up to a standing position and grabbed a tree trunk to steady herself.

Kelly blinked her eyes, forcing them to stay open by sheer force of will. It wouldn't take a rocket scientist to figure out that she needed to find shelter while she was still conscious. Temperatures were dropping every minute. There had to be a place she could hide and lie low until the effects of the contents of that glass wore off.

The minute she gave in to darkness and blacked out, any wild animal—coyote, bear or hog—could come along and use her as an easy meal.

Keeping a clear head was getting more difficult. Darkness nipped at her even though the sun shone brightly through the trees. She had no idea what had really been in that drink or how much longer she could fight it off.

At least she'd stopped the man in the tuxedo, aka Tux, from giving her the entire glass like he'd threatened to do, like he'd tried. Her quick thinking and action—a sharp knee to the groin—was the only reason she could still function. Otherwise, she'd be splayed across the velvet sofa, pliant. *Dead?*

That swift knee to Tux's groin had put a halt to those plans.

Was he trying to subdue her or kill her? To what end? What could Tux possibly have gained from either?

Her first thought was sexual motivation, but for reasons she couldn't explain she knew that wasn't right.

Figuring out exactly who Tux was and what he wanted would have to wait until her mind was clear again. There was another threat closing in. It felt like it wasn't more than a few feet behind her, gaining ground.

Trees were thickening and the underbrush felt like hands gripping her legs, stopping her from forward progress.

Was there anything or anyone around? Could she shout for help? Or would that draw the wrong kind of attention?

Fear that Tux would be the only one to respond kept her quiet as she dredged through the thicket. Her body was getting weaker, she was moving slower.

What was in that drink?

Rohypnol? She'd read about the date-rape drug being used rampantly on college campuses.

Kelly leaned on a tree's sturdy trunk to stay upright as her body trembled and she tried to shake the overwhelming feeling of doom as it enveloped her.

THE WORDS *HIGH ALERT* didn't begin to describe the mood at the Kent family ranch as Will Kent walked his horse, Domino, along the fence on the northeastern border of the property. A few days ago, one of the heifers was found near the base of Rushing Creek. Her front left hoof had been cut off, mangled. As disgusting as that act was, it didn't end her life immediately. From the looks of her when she'd been found, she'd been left to bleed to death.

Will couldn't allow himself to believe the killer had stuck around and watched, although speculation about what had happened was running wild. Jacobstown was a small, tight-knit community that had seen little crime.

Thinking about the incident caused Will's trapezoids to tense. His shoulder muscles were strung tight to the point of pain. It didn't help matters that his older brother, Mitch, and his wife had been targeted by criminals and had narrowly escaped, as well. Thankfully, Mitch, Kimberly and their twins were safe. The jerks who'd been tormenting Kimberly were securely locked behind bars.

A year had passed since that incident, and there was no sign that the person or group who'd brutally killed one of his heifers planned to return. The Kents didn't leave much to chance. They decided to remain vigilant, anyway. As far as they were concerned the threat to the herd still loomed.

Life was beginning to return to normal around the ranch. And normal for a rancher meant up by 4:00 a.m. every day. Will suppressed a yawn. Early mornings had been always been Mitch's thing, not Will's. He'd never been a morning person. His night-owl tendencies were being pushed to their limits since moving back to the ranch to work full-time.

Will, like everyone in his family, was paying extra attention to the threat to their livestock. So far, only one heifer had been affected, but who knew where this would ultimately end. Their cousin, Zach McWilliams, was the sheriff and he had no leads in the case, which had horrified and disturbed the bedroom community of Jacobstown. He tugged at the collar of his shirt.

Anger caused Will's shoulder blades to lock up. Hurting an innocent animal, whether out of ignorance or blatant torture, was right up there on the list of things Will would never tolerate. Especially not animals in his and his family's trust.

The Kent family fortune had been made from owning thousands of acres of land across Texas and the accompanying mineral rights. Their mother, the matriarch, had passed away four years ago and their father nearly two years later. Will and his siblings had inherited the ranch and all its holdings, and were sewing up other business pursuits as each made his or her way to living on the land full-time.

Will circled the base of Rushing Creek again in order to cover the area one more time. Normally being out on the land brought a sense of peace. Not today. Not since the heifer.

Other than the occasional and rare prank of cow tipping, the ranch was normally a peaceful place and Jacobstown would be considered a sleepy town by most people's standards. The kind where everyone was on a first name basis, a handshake was considered similar to a legal document and the streets rolled up by eight o'clock every night. Will ran his finger along the shirt of his collar again, needing a little more breathing room.

He took in a deep breath, trying to breathe a sense of calm into his soul. He was restless. Had been since the heifer. Longer than that if he was being honest. Analyzing himself like a shrink wasn't at the top of his list. Protecting the herd was, however, and he was all-in when it came to the animals on his family land.

A streak of white caught his eye in the distance. He couldn't see clearly between the trees and it was most likely nothing. But he turned his horse toward the object, anyway.

As Domino moved closer to the area, Will could see more movement. The white figure was zigzagging between trees and he could tell someone was on the move. A woman?

He nudged Domino into a trot. At the faster pace, the person was no match for his horse, even as he slowed his horse enough to wind through the thickening trees.

"Stop!" Will shouted, not wanting to surprise the person. He was close enough to see that the material was expensive and was wedding-dress white. It was some type of gown that trailed behind her as she whipped in and out of the trees. The cloud-puff-looking garment alternated between the trees, flowing behind her. The scene was something out of a bride's magazine and was oddly mesmerizing. It also caused his chest to squeeze.

She kept running, which made her look guilty of something quite frankly. He doubted she was responsible for the heifer but she was up to something or she would have stopped when he called out to her. Innocent people didn't run.

The trees slowed Domino's pace as he wound through the tall oaks and mesquites that were abundant as they tracked White Dress.

There was something frantic about her pace and the way she zigzagged through the woods. Was she running from someone besides him?

Nah. He shook off the possibility.

"Hold on there." He decided to take a different tack and intentionally softened his voice. "Do you need help?"

Domino's pace slowed to a crawl as the woods thickened near the eastern fencing. Kent land stretched miles beyond this area. Where did White Dress think she was going?

"Whoa," Will said to his horse.

Domino's size was getting in the way of being

nimble enough to catch her. At this point, Will could walk faster.

He climbed off his horse and tied Domino to a tree. He patted his gelding. “This shouldn’t take long. I’ll be right back, buddy.”

From behind, he could see that White Dress was five-and-a-half-feet tall, give or take. As he moved closer, he saw streaks of red on her dress. Blood? Was she hurt?

Her warm brown hair with streaks of honey looked more like a galloping horse’s mane, shiny and flowing as the wind whipped it around.

“Slow down. I have no plans to hurt you,” he said.

She glanced back at him and the look on her face was a punch to his gut. There was so much desperation and fear.

As he got closer, he could see that she wore a short-sleeved lacy wedding dress that fell just below the knee and a pair of dress boots with an intricate teal inlay. Will was gaining on her but not because he was increasing his speed. White Dress was slowing down and she seemed to be stumbling over her boots a little bit. His mind took a different turn. Was she under the influence of something?

She grabbed onto a tree trunk before glancing back at him. She was just far enough ahead for him to barely make out the details of her face. The woman was a looker with those hauntingly beautiful eyes. There was no argument about that. She held onto that tree like gravity would shoot her into the clouds if she let go.

"Who are you?" Will asked again, using the softer tone. She wore the expression of a frightened animal as she made another run for it.

White Dress's boot must've caught on something because she vaulted forward and narrowly missed planting the crown of her head against an oak tree's trunk when she landed. She popped up onto all fours and tried to scramble away. Her movements were awkward and wobbly, causing more questions to flood him. Had she hit her head? Had she lost a lot of blood and was about to pass out?

Then again, she might've been drinking and gotten hurt. He'd seen more than a few instances of hormone-infused good-ol'-boy drinking and the ensuing antics.

Growing up on the family ranch, he'd seen everything from cow-tipping to the south pasture accidentally catching on fire because of a gang of intoxicated teens. They'd claimed to be unaware the state was in a drought when they'd decided to roast hot dogs on a campfire at three o'clock in the morning after sneaking out.

"Look. I'm not going to hurt you so you might as well stop and tell me what you're doing on my family's land." This time, he let his frustration seep in his tone. He didn't have time for this. It was getting late in the day and he needed to head back to the ranch.

White Dress seemed determined to get away from him. He'd give her that. So, he jogged ahead of her and turned around to face her.

Those violet eyes of hers—filled with an interesting mix of sheer determination and panic—fixated on him as she managed to stumble to her feet and hold onto another tree trunk.

"We can do this for as long as you'd like. But you're on my land and I'm not going anywhere until I know why you're here and that you'll leave safely." He stood in an athletic stance, ready to take action the second she bolted.

"Then help me." Her words slurred and for another split second he wondered if she'd been drinking.

"Tell me your name and I'll see what I can do." He fished out his cell, keeping an eye on her. For all he knew her tipsiness could be an act and she could take off again once he was distracted.

She hesitated. Her grip on the tree trunk was white-knuckled.

"My name's Will Kent." He figured a little goodwill would go a long way toward winning her trust. She had that frightened-animal look that came right before a bite. A scared animal could do a lot of damage.

On closer look, she seemed familiar. Did he know her?

"I know who you are. I'm Kelly Morgan," she finally said and there was a resignation in her tone that made him inclined to believe she was telling the truth. Her facial expression wasn't so defeated and he knew instantly that she would take any out that presented itself.

"Are you supposed to be somewhere, Mrs. Morgan?" He glanced at the white dress and then his eyes immediately flew to the ring finger on her left hand to see if the wedding had already taken place. There was nothing.

She shook her head almost violently.

"I'm not. I mean, I know what this must look like but—" Again her words were slurred.

She followed his gaze to the dress and her face paled.

"Are you hurt?" he asked, focusing on the long red streaks of blood.

"I don't think so," she said in a panicked tone as she ran her hands along the beading of her dress at her midsection.

His thoughts instantly skipped to the possibility that she'd had a few shots of "liquid courage" before she ended up chickening out and splitting on her wedding day. The thought of the man she'd left behind, another human being, standing at an altar somewhere and waiting—like an idiot!—for a woman who would never show stuck in Will's craw. He tensed at the possibility. No man deserved to have his hopes trampled like that.

Will bit back what he really wanted to say.

"Today your wedding day?" he asked in an even tone as memories he'd tucked away down deep clawed to the surface.

"No." She looked bewildered. "But it's not safe for me. I have to keep going."

She aimed herself at another tree and more or less threw her body toward it, grasping at the trunk.

"*Whoa*. Steady there," Will said, stepping toward her to catch her elbow and hold her upright.

She mumbled an apology and something that sounded like she was saying she'd been drugged.

Did he hear her right?

This close, he could see the unique violet color in her irises, and when he looked deeper there was something else that would haunt him for the rest of his days—a split second of unadulterated fear.

Did she think he was going to hurt her?

"I'll help you get this sorted out," he said to reassure her, thinking this day was turning into a doozy.

"Why did he…? What did he…?"

Did she know where she was?

Even sounding confused, there was a musical quality to her voice.

It dawned on him what had been bugging him.

He knew that name.

Chapter Two

Kelly Morgan. Will remembered that name from somewhere. *Where?*

As inappropriate as the thought seemed under the circumstances, he figured that he'd know if he'd met a woman *this* beautiful before.

After a few seconds, he realized how he knew her. The two of them had gone to grade school together. They'd been nothing more than kids. Damn, the memory of her reached back into his childhood. And to be fair, the Kelly Morgan he'd known was a tall, scrawny girl. Not a woman who'd filled out in sexy, soft-looking curves.

Being from a small town, he'd prided himself on having history with darn near all local families, but hers had kept to themselves. Kelly had had a quiet but strong quality even then.

And then the summer after fifth grade the family was gone. Years later, he'd heard that they'd relocated to Fort Worth for her dad's work. Even now Will remembered looking for her that first day of middle school. There was something about the young

Kelly that had brought out his protective instincts back then. Was the same thing happening now, too?

Kelly Morgan could take care of herself. Still, he recalled the almost too-thin girl who liked to sit by the window in the back of the room. She'd had a serious quality—too serious for her age. To this day it made him wonder where it came from and why.

"Tell me what's going on and I'll help," he said, the memory softening his tone.

He needed to get her back to Domino before she passed out. In her state he couldn't be sure the blood on her gown wasn't hers. She might be hurt and not realize it.

His horse was a fifteen-minute walk from this part of Rushing Creek. He knew the land like the back of his hand, having grown up here.

Kelly took another step back and had to tighten her grip on the tree trunk to keep her balance.

"Tell me what's going on. What happened to you?" he asked, but her eyes darted around frantically.

"He did this… I don't know what he gave me," she said hesitantly. He was close enough to see her pulse pounding rapidly at the base of her throat—a throat he had no business noticing…the soft angles or how silky the skin seemed.

Was this a simple case of woman who'd had too much to drink and ditched her fiancé on her wedding day? That wouldn't explain the blood. She looked frightened and he wanted to believe it could be that simple. His survival skills, which had been honed in combat, made him think otherwise.

Why would she come into the woods? And what was she talking about? "What did he give you?"

He leaned in, close enough to pick up the scent of alcohol on her breath if it was there. There was no smell. Being this close to her stirred something inappropriate, though, and it was completely out of line given the situation.

Great job, Will. Way to keep yourself in check.

"Lean your weight on me," he urged, trying to forget the familiar pain that came from seeing someone running in the opposite direction in a wedding dress.

Had Lacey had this same frantic, pained look on her face on their wedding day? Two years had passed, which should have been enough time to tuck away the memories and forget the whole thing had ever happened. Most of the time that was a no-brainer. Done. Then there were moments like these.

Will Kent had lived a charmed life. Until Lacey had crushed his heart with the heel of her boot. He bit back a bitter laugh. Wasn't he being dramatic? It was most likely the fact that the anniversary of what was supposed to be their wedding was coming up in a couple of days.

A noise to Will's left nearly caused Kelly to bolt like a motherless doe.

"Shhh," he whispered. Her reaction heightened his awareness of their surroundings. Her emotions were on high alert and would be overkill for a woman who was solely ducking out on vows. The blood on her dress said there was more to the story.

"Pleas-s-s-e don't let him hur-l me," she said, slurring the words. Did she mean *hurt*? He assumed so.

He scanned the area before catching her eye. He brought his right index finger to his lips, indicating silence.

She unfocused her gaze for a few seconds, like she was looking into herself for answers. Then she blinked before locking onto something in the distance behind him.

Will jerked his head around in time to hear the crack of a gun going off, followed by the unmistakable sound of a bullet pinging off the tree next to him. His eyes immediately followed the sound and saw that the tree trunk had a chunk missing. That was about two feet from his head. His gaze flew in the direction of the gun.

A short man with a slight build who wore jeans and a dark hoodie was bolting toward them, shotgun barrel seeking a better look at its target.

There was no time for debate so he picked up Kelly and darted in between the trees running a zigzag pattern as fast as he could. Work on the ranch had kept him in solid shape, so he could push hard without being winded.

Kelly couldn't have been wearing a worse color to blend in with the surroundings and to make matters worse her billowy dress bounced and trailed behind them with every step. The breeze toyed with the sinless white material. Her long wavy ringlets blocked his vision and he didn't want to take in her scent even though it blasted through him, anyway. She smelled like flowers and sunshine on the first warm day of spring, when everything bloomed.

There were half a dozen questions zinging through his mind demanding a response. Answers would have to wait until the two of them were out of danger. He also had a flash of panic that the blood on her dress meant she'd been shot.

Will ducked as another bullet splintered a piece of bark a couple yards away. Thick trees would make getting a clean shot next to impossible and that played to his advantage.

Keeping a calm head no matter the circumstances had always been his strong suit.

Will ran through the situation in his mind as he zipped through the tall trees.

Based on aim, this guy wasn't a stellar marksman, which played to Will's advantage. A shotgun wasn't accurate but the bullet spray might do a lot more damage at this distance. There'd be shell pieces within a range of twenty feet this far away from the shooter. There was a reason it was called buckshot and it spread shrapnel across a decent distance.

The other advantage Will had over the shooter was knowledge of the property. No one knew this area better than a Kent and Will was no exception.

Will weaved through the trees. His speed and sheer willpower kept him a good distance from the shooter. This guy didn't seem to be a match for Will's athleticism and he appreciated the fact that Kelly wasn't fighting against him. He could also thank years of sports in high school and his stint in the military for his fitness. Being used to a daily training routine had him waking up every morning at three o'clock to get in a workout before eating a protein-heavy breakfast and heading out to work an hour later.

The beauty in his arms seemed to be struggling to stay alert. With every few feet of progress, she shook her head or blinked her eyes. She muttered a couple of apologies and he assumed she meant she was sorry for him having to carry her. Although, he couldn't be sure.

Adrenaline caused Will to run faster. The shooter might not be a great marksman but all it took was one hit for this game of chase to be over. Will knew how to handle the extra power surge that came with adrenaline and he was accustomed to managing the extra cortisol coursing through his body by measuring his breaths to keep them even.

He knew what it was like to have bullets flying past his head and seemingly no easy outs. A smile threatened to crack his lips because a part of him missed the adrenaline rushes that came with his time during combat. The other part of being away from home and coming back to the States in time for his fiancée to ditch him on their wedding day—that had been a humdinger.

Will was good at combat. Real life? Not so much.

Even though he'd grown up in a close-knit family he'd never been one to linger on emotions.

Being left at the altar when he'd believed he and his fiancée were in love showed him just how far off base he'd been. It didn't seem to matter how many people told him to forget about her. That she wasn't worth the trouble. He tried to tell that to the beating blob of blood and tissue in the center of his chest. Damn thing had a mind of its own.

Hell, he knew his family was right about Lacey. And normally he'd walk away and never look back. He had a weakness for the woman that defied logic. Or did it? A twinge of guilt pinched his gut. He most definitely felt protective of his ex.

That same protective instinct flared with the woman in his arms and it struck him that he was walking down a path he'd gone down before. Or, in this case, running was more like it, as he dodged another bullet that struck a tree a little too close for comfort.

Keep this up much longer and the law of probability said that even a bad shot would hit his target given enough time and opportunity.

Will needed a plan.

As far as he could tell he was dealing with a lone shooter. His own shotgun was strapped to Domino.

An old treehouse was up ahead around a hill. Maybe he could make it there.

Dodging in and out of trees was slowing his pace. Carrying Kelly was no problem after doing the same for a wounded soldier wearing sixty pounds of gear through mountainous terrain in hundred-plus temperatures.

Of course, he was older now and not nearly in the

same shape. His stamina wouldn't hold out as long. All those factors had to be considered.

Getting to Domino safely without risking a wild shot hitting his horse was risky.

Will didn't like it, but his only option was to get Kelly out of the woods and to the medical attention she needed. The slurred speech might be caused by blood loss.

But then what? an annoying voice in the back of his mind asked.

STAY AWAKE. STAYING ALERT was Kelly's highest priority. She hated being in this position, feeling like a victim. There was nothing worse than a feeling of helplessness, but it was taking all the strength she had inside her to stay awake and fight the darkness weighing down her thoughts.

Her mind zinged back to when she was a teenager. It had been two days since her thirteenth birthday had officially ushered her into her teen years. Kelly woke with a cramp in her side that made her double over and left her rocking back and forth in pain.

Her mother walked in after working her shift at the hair salon and gasped when she saw her daughter on the floor. Her appendix had almost burst and she'd been cramping so hard she could barely walk.

"Why didn't you call me?" her mother had asked.

"I thought it would pass," Kelly said weakly, in between blowing out breaths to try and manage her pain. She'd done everything she could think of in order to distract herself.

Before she could blow out her next breath, her mother was helping Kelly to her feet.

"I'm taking you to the hospital," she'd stated and Kelly had heard the panic in her mother's voice. She had immediately known that she must have looked awful based on her mother's expression.

After her mother had managed to get her buckled into the passenger seat of the family sedan, Kelly saw how much her mother's hands were shaking on the wheel. It took three tries for her to get the key into the ignition. Her mother let out a few choice words, glanced her daughter's way and apologized, before finally finding the hole and starting the engine.

Kelly must've been in bad shape because her mother kept repeating, "Stay with me, baby."

Pain threatened to drag Kelly under and hold her in the current, pulling her further out to sea. Then there were tires squealing as her mother stomped on the brakes in the ER bay. The sun was out, brightening the sky, and would be for hours before plunging into the western landscape. It was an unusually hot afternoon even for August in Texas.

People rushed toward them and then Kelly was being placed on a gurney and wheeled into the hospital. She remembered the rectangles on the ceiling and the bright fluorescent lights. The sound of doors opening and closing while a male voice shouted orders.

She didn't remember how long the nurse told her she'd been out when she woke from surgery. There was a recovery room and the strangeness of fading in and out. And then suddenly her mother was there.

It didn't strike her as odd at first that her father was nowhere to be seen. It should have, because he was the family's rock. Her first thought was that he'd been held up in traffic. Then she'd realized it was Sunday—Sundays were for fishing.

There shouldn't be any traffic. But still, she reasoned that it would take time to dock the boat and load it onto the platform before driving the boat home. Would he go straight home to drop off the boat? Based on her mother's panicked expression, Kelly thought he would rush straight to the hospital.

There was no sign of her brother, either.

And then it dawned on her that an eight-year-old most likely wouldn't be allowed near the surgery area. Her dad was probably in the waiting room with Kellan, feeding a vending machine a few quarters to give him a snack. Her brother had been on a growth spurt and there wasn't enough food to keep that child satisfied lately.

"Hi, baby," her mother had said and then her chin had quivered. Her voice was shaky.

Before Kelly could respond, her mother burst into tears.

"What's wrong?" The words finally came. Her mouth was as dry as west Texas soil in a drought, so she choked when she tried to speak.

Her mother shook her head. "I'm sorry."

Her words were strained and a knot immediately formed in Kelly's stomach. She thought there was something terribly wrong with her, like the doctor had found an incurable disease.

And then a few moments later, when her mom said the words that changed both of their lives forever, her father and baby brother had been killed in an accident on the way to the hospital to see her.

Kelly wished she was the one to die.

All Kelly remembered was rolling onto her side and crying herself to sleep. She didn't want to wake up. Didn't want to get out of bed. It was as if a heavy weight pressed down her limbs, her body. She was powerless. Helpless.

It had been the worst feeling in the world.

Another bullet pegged a tree near Kelly's head, shocking her thoughts back to the present.

Anger roared through her. No one got to make her feel that way again.

She cringed and gripped the cowboy as tightly as she could. He was strong and fast, but not even he could run forever while carrying her.

He was zigzagging through the woods, sometimes making a turn just in the nick of time to dodge a bullet.

His fluid movements and ability to cut left or right like momentum didn't exist reminded her of the best cutting horse she'd ever seen. Denny.

If anything happened to him she'd be to blame.

"Put me down and get out of here," she squeaked out. Her heart couldn't take another person dying because of her.

"What?" The cowboy was barely winded.

"No sheriff."

She tried to form more words but darkness silenced her.

Chapter Three

Will bolted through the property, carrying dead weight in his arms.

Kelly's body had gone limp.

The shooter had disappeared.

Will rounded the base of Horseshoe Trail, a popular riding trail among visitors to the ranch.

Kelly's last words spoken before she lost consciousness perplexed him. Why no sheriff? There was a man trying to kill her and now, by extension, him. Hell yes, he was calling the sheriff. Zach McWilliams was not only a damn fine lawman, but he was also Will's cousin. They'd grown up close. Zach had spent a good bit of his childhood on the ranch and every summer he'd come to live with them while his parents worked. He was more like a brother than cousin and that's exactly how Will knew he could be trusted.

Innocent people didn't run from the law, but there was nothing else about Kelly that made him think she was a criminal. Either way, he wanted to get to safety and find out what she was talking about before he made the call.

Figuring it was safe to circle back to Domino now, Will took a couple of right turns and made as little noise as possible as he navigated the journey toward his horse.

Carrying Kelly for the past hour caused his arms to burn. Domino was a good twenty-minute walk from Will's current location. The walk would give him time to clear his head and focus on his next move.

He wasn't on the hike five minutes when his cell vibrated in his pocket. He balanced the woman in his arms, using a tree as a foundation, then slipped a hand in his jeans pocket and fished out his phone. He hit the green button with his thumb before cradling the phone against his shoulder.

"Got a strange visitor today." Will instantly recognized the voice of his older brother, Mitch.

That didn't sound good.

"Oh, yeah? Who?" he asked.

"A woman stopped by and said her friend was missing. She wanted to know if any of us had seen her and then in a blast-from-the-past move she held up a picture of Kelly Morgan." Shock didn't begin to describe Will's reaction.

"Do you remember her from school?" Mitch asked.

"I have her right here in my arms," Will admitted. "She's wearing a wedding dress and a man with a gun was chasing her when I ran into her near the base of Rushing Creek."

"Are you okay?" Mitch's concern came through clearly.

"So far, so good, but the shooter could still be out here." Rushing Creek had seen a little too much action considering his brother had found the dead heifer near the exact same spot where Will found Kelly.

"What's going on? Did she say?" Mitch asked before it seemed to dawn on him that Will had said she was in his arms. "Did you say you're carrying her?"

"That's right. She conked out after asking me not to call Zach," Will informed him.

"What about the man with the gun? Did she run out on him before their wedding?" Mitch was trying to piece together the story. Heck if Will could fill in his brother.

"He didn't ask questions before he started shooting," Will said.

His brother bit out a few expletives. "You sure you're okay?"

"I'm fine. She has blood on her dress and the guy's loose on the property," he said. "I'm on my way back to Domino where I tied him off."

"I'll call Zach."

"Before Kelly passed out she warned me about bringing in the law," Will revealed.

"Zach? What could she possibly be talking about? He's honest and there's no better investigator in the state."

"We both know that but I guess she hasn't figured it out. I'm scratching my head but I imagine she has her reasons," Will said. "I didn't pick up any signs of alcohol on her breath, but I have to admit she was acting odd when I found her. Then a guy shows up with a gun and starts shooting. No one's stopping to ask questions. I grabbed her and took off."

"Is she hurt?" Mitch issued a sharp breath. His brother wouldn't like anything about this situation.

"There's not enough blood for her to still be bleeding," Will said after taking stock.

"Sounds like she needs a doctor, anyway," Mitch said and Will agreed.

"I'd like to keep all this under the radar until we know exactly who and what we're dealing with," Will said.

"You already know I'll help any way I can." Will's older brother had never let him down.

"I know." He heard a branch-snapping noise to the east so he lowered his voice when he said, "I'm not out of the woods yet."

"Where are you now?"

Will provided his general location and where he'd left his horse.

"Hold on. I'm sending men your way right now to secure the area," Mitch said. "I'll get Dr. Carter to the house and Zach on the line. We'll figure this out."

"I don't want to endanger anyone unnecessarily," Will warned.

"How's Kelly's breathing?" Mitch asked.

Will dropped his gaze to her chest, doing his level

best to ignore her curves. Relief flooded him when he saw her chest rise and fall, steady and strong. "Seems good." He forced his gaze away from her full breasts, which were pressing against the sheer white of her dress.

"We'll seal off the area. Make sure this guy can't get to the house or the casita," Mitch said.

"Make sure everyone's careful. This guy isn't a good aim but he's not afraid to pull the trigger and spray shells from here to Louisiana. Wish I'd gotten a better look at him so I could give a description," Will admitted.

"We can work with what we've got." Mitch paused. "He should be the only one out there aside from you since you were working alone today. Right?"

Will had thought about the possibility of others. "Can't be one-hundred-percent sure what we're dealing with. It's safer to assume there are more." His family was his rock and always had been. The Kent people were a close bunch and especially after losing both parents in the last four years. "I appreciate you."

"Goes without saying," Mitch acknowledged.

This land and this family were Will's life and had become the only two things he cared about since his ex had walked out. Even so, he'd been restless since returning from his tour. He figured it came with the territory. Leaving the military, where his life was literally on the line daily, and returning to a quiet civilian life had seemed like a good plan. Get back to nature. Get his bearings again. Be normal. But things had changed. *He'd* changed. He hadn't quite gotten his footing yet.

"The minute she wakes I'll find out what I can," Will stated, still on a whisper so as not to draw unwanted attention.

"Zach will need anything we can give him to work with," Mitch agreed. "Be careful out there until we can get you some backup."

"Will do."

"Love you, man," Mitch said before he ended the call on a similar sentiment.

Fifteen minutes after the conversation with his brother, Will came upon the spot where he'd left Domino.

The horse was gone.

KELLY BLINKED HER eyes open. She felt woozy and disoriented as she pushed up on her elbows.

Fear seized her as she realized it was pitch black and she had no idea where she was or what she was doing there.

"You awake?" A familiar male voice sent a shiver of awareness through her.

She didn't respond because warning bells also sounded.

He must've realized she was scared beyond belief because he added, "It's Will Kent. I found you on my ranch about an hour ago."

She searched her memory… *Will Kent?* The wealthy kid she remembered from grade school? What on earth would she be doing with him? An image of a large man wearing a tuxedo rippled panic through her.

"What are you wearing?" she said in a whisper. Her voice was raspy.

"What?" He sounded bewildered but she needed to know.

"Clothes. What do you have on?" she choked out.

There was a moment of silence before a sharp breath issued. "Well, let's see. I have on jeans and a T-shirt."

Tux was definitely not Will Kent. Relief was a flood to dry plains.

"Where am I?" she whispered.

"In a casita on my family's land. I'd open a curtain or turn on a light but we can't risk being discovered until help arrives." His voice brought a sense of calm over her she knew better than to trust.

She strained to remember but it felt like someone had poured concrete inside her skull and it had hardened.

"Why am I here?" she finally asked, hating that she sounded scared.

"You tell me," the strong masculine voice said. The deep timbre reverberated down her spine, sending sensual tingles behind it. Her reactions were totally inappropriate to the situation and she mentally chided herself for them.

"Mind if I come closer?" Will asked.

She felt around her body to see if she was wearing clothes and was relieved to find that she was.

But then she couldn't imagine a man like Will Kent taking advantage of her.

"Okay," she said.

She was being cautious but that was silly because a voice inside her told her that she could trust this man. And then the memory of the tuxedo man flashed in her thoughts. Fear was a living, breathing entity growing inside her. The overbearing smell of piney aftershave hit her—Tux's aftershave. It had burned her nose and threatened to overwhelm her again just thinking about it.

She gripped her stomach to stave off nausea.

The mattress dipped next to her but she felt his male presence as he walked across the room toward her.

She should be afraid. Instead, warmth blanketed her.

This wasn't the time to remember the crush she'd had on Will Kent in grade school, or that being near him now brought certain feelings to life. As a grown woman she didn't do childish fantasies and it felt silly that her cheeks flamed with him this close despite her internal admonishment.

Apparently, reason flew out the window as soon as a hot cowboy entered the picture. Will was more than a good-looking face with a body made for sin, though. He was intelligent but careful. He'd always been a little quiet and intense, which only made him more attractive in her eyes.

Will seemed the kind of man who stood by his

principles and didn't seem to see the need to move his lips unless there was purpose.

"Are you taking medication?" he asked.

"What?" She didn't bother to hide her shock at his question.

"You seemed out of it when I found you—loopy. And at first, I thought you'd been drinking with it being your wedding day and—"

"Hold on right there. My *what*?"

Chapter Four

Kelly's reaction threw off Will. But then she seemed to be having a day if ever there was one. "You're wearing a wedding dress. It seems to fit. I assumed you meant to put it on. So, I'm guessing it's your wedding day."

"I put that much together for myself but I have no idea what I'm doing in this getup," she admitted. If she was lying she was damn good at it.

"You're Will Kent," she added.

"That's right."

"We were in grade school together," she said.

"Right again." His phone buzzed, indicating a text message. He cupped the screen to block light so as not to make it act as a beacon, and checked the message.

"The sheriff is outside."

He texted back, letting his cousin know the two of them were in position and alone as far as he knew. Zach would take extra precaution so as not to bring the shooter to their doorstep. The last thing anyone wanted was a shootout. A text informing him that

Domino had been found spooked but unharmed had come forty-five minutes ago and was a welcome relief. Thoughts of his horse being butchered like the heifer had anger brewing inside him.

He glanced up. His eyes had long ago adjusted to the dark. He could see Kelly's outline and she was making a move to stand.

"Whoa. Hold on there." In the next second he was by her side, steadying her and stopping her from taking a fall.

Physical contact sent more unexpected and unwelcomed currents of electricity thrumming through his veins. It hadn't been *that* long since he'd been with a woman. An annoying voice in the back of his mind reminded him that it had been too long since he'd been with one who caused that kind of reaction from him. The thought was about as productive as drinking a shot of whiskey after eating a ghost pepper.

"I can't stay here," she said and her voice was shaky.

"Why not?" He remembered that she'd warned him against bringing in the law. "Are you involved in something illegal?"

"No." She took a step and her knee gave.

Will pulled her in tighter, ignoring the shot of electricity.

"Thank you," she said and her voice was laced with emotion. He didn't need to see clearly to know that she was crying and it caused his heart to squeeze. Whatever was going on, she was in a fix and he found himself wanting to help. Then again, his blood was pumping for the first time since returning to the ranch. He couldn't ignore the possibility that being shot at a little while ago was the first time he'd felt alive since leaving the military. Readjusting to the real world, when he'd been damn good at being a soldier, was proving harder than he expected. Thinking about it caused the restless feeling to return.

Those were dangerous thoughts so he shoved them down deep.

"Hang in there. Help is almost here," he reassured Kelly as she leaned more of her weight against him. The soft curve of her hip came up to the outside of his upper thigh and lit a thousand fires at the point of contact.

His hands felt a little too right on her as he shouldered more of her weight. He told himself that he needed to call Renee back. She'd been after him for a date since her friend's New Year's Eve shindig. Will had gone to the party out of boredom and found himself even more restless among the dancing and boozing. He was definitely off-kilter. The old Will would've enjoyed a night with a pretty woman. But that was before Lacey had left him at the altar and shredded his heart. He'd tried to convince himself that he wasn't over her, but that wasn't true, either. Being burned still stung, but part of him had known he and Lacey had been making a mistake.

Being on the ranch was supposed to provide the answers he searched for. So far, he'd just counted cattle and shoveled manure. Busy work kept his mind from spinning out.

Will moved to the door, maintaining a slow pace so that Kelly could keep up. He situated her so that she could lean against the wall as he texted Zach. The rescue team was in position. He and Kelly were stationed and ready to go.

The doorknob jiggled.

Even knowing who was on the other side didn't stop the familiar—and comforting?—adrenaline rush from thrumming through him, awakening all that had been dead. There had been one too many times that he felt like one of his parents, or both, would come walking through the kitchen door of the main house since his return. He needed to get it through his thick skull that both were gone.

Within a couple of minutes Will and Kelly were being guided out of the woods and ushered toward the main house.

Kelly had that frightened-deer expression, her violet eyes wild.

He tightened his grip around her waist in a move of silent reassurance as he led her into the house, then to the living room and onto the sofa, where he gently placed her.

Dr. Carter, a longtime family friend, went to work. The man was in his early sixties and had the face of a weathered grandfather. He had a medium build and kept himself in shape with a competitive cycling club. He was average height, had medium brown hair and a prominent nose. In his office there were enough degrees and accolades hanging on the wall to litter a small town. The doc was the best.

"Thanks for coming on short notice," Will said with a handshake.

The doc smiled, then sanitized his hands and put on a pair of gloves. He took a knee beside Kelly. "I can see that you're in pain. On a scale of one to ten, how much does it hurt?"

"A solid seven," she said in between breaths. Those huge violet eyes of hers outlined her panic.

Will rounded the coffee table and perched on the edge, opposite the doctor. Kelly reached for Will's hand and issued a sharp breath with the move.

"I'll be able to give you something to help with that pain when I'm finished with the exam," the doc assured her.

"Okay." Kelly's shoulders tensed as he dabbed what Will could only guess was some type of cleaning agent on her wound. Her chin came up and he admired her strength. His heart pitched and he reminded himself not to notice these things about her. Soon enough, she'd be whisked away to the hospital and would be out of his life.

EMTs were pulling up outside as Zach came through the front door. Deputies Lorenzano and Peabody were outside standing guard, after having rushed Kelly and Will to the main house.

Will turned and caught a look from his cousin.

"Do you remember Kelly Morgan from elementary school?" Will asked.

Zach shook his head.

Will motioned toward her. Zach had been two grades behind them, so it wasn't a shock that he didn't remember her.

"We were classmates. Haven't seen her since her family moved away from Jacobstown in fifth grade," he said by way of explanation.

"I just got a call about an abandoned vehicle," Zach warned. "The owner is missing."

"We can all see that I'm right here," Kelly said as she winced.

For the second time, Zach shook his head. "I'm sorry, but the name the car is registered to is Christina Foxwood."

Kelly took in a sharp breath. "She's my cousin."

"When did you last see her?" Zach asked.

Kelly seemed to search her memory. "I can't remember."

"Is it safe to say that it's been a long time?" Zach had a notepad out, and was jotting down a few notes.

"No. We live in the same building." She massaged her temples as though that might stimulate her thoughts. "I know I've seen her, I just don't remember where or when. I also know that I was forced to drink something and it's playing havoc with my memory. There was a man. I mean, he's so hazy but I feel like there was a guy in a tux trying to hurt me. I struggled and got away from him but things are hazy. I feel dizzy and like I might vomit."

"But you remembered me," Will stated.

She nodded. "When I saw you. You seemed familiar, so I searched my brain and came up with the connection."

"Do you have any idea where your cousin might be right now?" Zach asked.

"Not really."

"Have the two of you spoken to each other?" Zach asked and Will figured his cousin persisted with the line of questions to see if he could spur something in Kelly.

"This can't be happening." She had that bewildered look Will had seen earlier when he'd first found her. "Who reported her missing?"

"We know that her abandoned vehicle was found on the side of the road alongside the Jasper property two hours ago. There was blood splattered inside the vehicle." He held up a hand, as though in surrender. "We don't know who it belongs to. I put a call in for help from neighboring counties. My deputies are processing the scene but that'll take time." He shot a glance toward Will. "Keys were still in the ignition and the vehicle was left running with the passenger-side door open."

"She wouldn't just run off and leave her car on the side of the road," Kelly choked out in between sobs. She bent forward and clutched her stomach, as if she was staving off throwing up.

"I want you to take in a few slow breaths," Doc soothed, but Will was certain the comforting words fell on deaf ears.

Will moved next to her and, ignoring the sharp look from his cousin, put his arm around her shoulder. She repositioned underneath his arm and she felt a little too right there.

Zach's cell buzzed. He glanced at Will and Kelly.

"Excuse me," he said, before moving outside to the front porch.

"What is happening?" Kelly asked in between sobs.

"I'm not sure," Will said. "But we'll figure this out. We'll find Christina and whoever it was that drugged you."

Kelly looked up at him with those piercing violet eyes. "Promise?"

He nodded. Damned if he didn't know better than to make promises he couldn't keep. There was something about being with Kelly that made him feel grounded, connected for the first time since returning to Jacobstown. He needed to hold on to it.

A minute later, Zach stepped back into the room. "I just got a call from a Fort Worth businessman by the name of Fletcher Hardaway."

"What did *he* want?" she asked with a mix of shock and disdain in her voice.

"He's looking for his bride," Zach informed her. His gaze bounced from Kelly to Will.

Before Will could demand answers, Kelly turned to him with the most lost look in her eyes that he'd ever seen.

"I promise I have no idea what's going on but I'd know if I was supposed to get married," she said softly so he was the only one who heard. "Please, help me."

"Hardaway is under the impression that the two of you had plans to marry today." His cousin's words shouldn't have been a punch to the gut. Will's stomach lining took a hit, anyway.

He should stand up and walk away from this tangled mess. The feeling of being alive again won, against his better judgment.

"Stay here," he said to Kelly, pushing to his feet. He squared up with Zach. "Can we have a word outside?"

"I'm afraid not," Zach said. "That dress is evidence, she's a witness at the very least and I can't let her out of my sight."

THAT DRESS IS EVIDENCE. Those four words hit Kelly hard. They followed "she's a witness," and the sheriff's statement wouldn't have bothered her if it had stopped there. Kelly's instincts were screaming at her to get up and get the hell out of there.

The sheriff would stop her.

She already looked guilty without adding to her mounting problems.

Running would only make it worse. So, she fought her fight-or-flight instincts.

Christina was missing. Those words were daggers straight through her chest.

"There was a man in a tuxedo. He made me drink something. It was a clear liquid. He said it was water but it had this awful taste," she blurted out, figuring she needed to say something in her defense. Her gaze bounced from the sheriff to Will, searching for any signs that either one believed her. For some reason what Will thought especially mattered to her. "I spit it out and then he pushed me up against the wall. Hard. He pushed my head back and poured more of it down my throat. I managed to kick him, break away and run. Everything's hazy after that, and before is a total wash."

Will looked at Doc. "Is it strange that her short-term memory seems to be the problem?"

"It depends on what she was given," Doc Carter said.

"Do you remember where you were when that happened?" the sheriff asked. His voice told her that she wasn't doing a great job of convincing him.

"Had to be a wedding chapel. Right? I think I was in a bride's room but I swear I don't know why I'm the one in this dress." She pleaded with Will with her eyes. She met a wall of suspicion and it hurt.

"Can you stand?" the sheriff asked.

Will moved to her side and offered a hand up.

She took the offering, ignoring the frissons of heat from contact. They were more complications she didn't need to focus on right now.

Standing made her woozy. She almost took a tumble, but Will's hand wrapped around her waist to catch her. She had the fleeting thought that she wondered if the chemistry she felt pinging between them was real. Did he feel it? Those random thoughts had no place inside her head.

Christina was missing.

Kelly glanced down at the bloodstain on her white dress.

Someone was trying to kill her.

She'd trade places with her cousin in a beat because Christina hadn't turned up and she might be lying in a ditch or an alley somewhere.

Tears spilled down her cheeks.

"Thank you," she said to Will and her voice came out shaky. She chalked it up to overwrought emotions and whatever had been in the glass that Tux had given her.

None of this could be real.

Kelly prayed this was all a nightmare and she'd wake any second to find the world had righted itself again.

"What did the person who drugged you look like?" the sheriff asked and his voice was laced with sympathy. "Tell me everything you can remember. Hair color. Eyes. General size and shape."

"Tall. Built. He was linebacker-big but shorter. The rest of the details are fuzzy," she admitted. "He had darkish hair. I think. And he smelled like he'd taken a bath in aftershave. That much I remember distinctly. The scent was cheap, piney and overpowering."

Zach had taken out a pocket notebook and was writing down the few details she'd given him.

She knew it wasn't much to go on.

"Am I under arrest?" she asked.

"No, ma'am," the sheriff said but his serious tone didn't exactly cause warm and fuzzy feelings to rain down. "I will need to take that gown as evidence, though. I'd also like to have you checked out at the hospital."

"She'll need something warm to wear," Will stated. "She looks close enough to Amber's size. I'll find something in my sister's closet for Kelly. Everyone keeps clothes in the main house."

Will's face was like stone, hard and unreadable.

The doc finished his exam and declared that there was too much blood for all of it to belong to her and the small wound on her hip.

"There's blood spatter," he continued, "which isn't consistent with the type of injury she's sustained.

Will had already explained that everyone in the family kept clothes at the main house just in case the need to stay over arose. The reasoning usually included working too late to drive home.

A few moments later, Will returned with garments in hand.

Kelly released the breath she didn't realize she'd been holding.

"Is there somewhere I can change?" she asked, flashing her eyes at the sheriff. He'd been a child the last time she'd seen him. Strange how coming back made her think everyone would still be the same age as when she'd left town years ago. It was silly, she knew that. But in a strange way she'd half expected Zach McWilliams to still be in third grade, his younger sister, Amy, in preschool.

"Deputy Deloren can wait in the hall while you

change in the bathroom. Door'll have to stay open, of course," Zach said.

Panic gripped Kelly at the thought of a stranger watching her undress. She shot a wild look toward Will, whose forehead creased with concern.

He didn't speak.

Chapter Five

"To be clear. Whatever's going on legally with Kelly Morgan is none of my business," Will said to his cousin.

"No argument there." Zach nodded.

Will issued a loaded sigh. "I'll look after her while she changes."

Kelly turned so quickly, the hopeful look on her face shot a spear straight in the middle of Will's chest.

"I'll take it from here," Will said to Deputy Deloren.

The deputy looked to his boss for confirmation.

Zach studied Will for a long moment. And then he gave a nod.

Deputy Deloren held out an evidence bag and a pair of gloves. "Don't get your prints on the gown."

"They'll be on there already," Will said. "I had to carry her in the woods to get her to safety. She was in and out of consciousness."

He had the bloodstains on his shirt to prove it.

"Keep her in your sight at all times," Zach shouted as they rounded the corner into the hallway.

His cousin was taking a risk by allowing Will to accompany Kelly. Will knew that if anything happened, the move could easily cost Zach his job. The only reason Will had insisted was because he would never allow it to come to that. Still woozy, she wasn't going anywhere.

Will helped Kelly down the hall, ignoring the heat fizzing between them. He stopped at the door.

"Can you take it from here all right?" he asked.

She blinked up at him, those violet eyes wide and even more beautiful this close. His heart fisted when their gazes lingered. *Inappropriate* didn't begin to define the reaction he was having to Kelly. He did good to remind himself that she wore a wedding dress. Details of her life were sketchy at best.

She took in a sharp breath as she tried to move on her own. She stopped and he tucked a curly loose tendril of hair behind her ear.

"Did the guy wearing the tux hurt you in any way?" he asked her in the serious tone he used when he was trying to keep from hitting someone. He wanted five minutes alone with the guy in the tux who'd put those marks on her back.

She cocked her head to the side and it was sexy as hell.

"Aside from what you already told us. Did he put a hand on you?" Will asked through clenched teeth. He had half a mind to hunt down the man himself and spend a couple of minutes outlining why a person shouldn't pick on someone smaller. Although, she'd given the guy hell, and a feeling of pride Will had no right to own welled in his chest.

This close, he could see her pulse racing, thumping at the base of her throat.

Kelly didn't speak. Instead, she bit her lip and slowly shook her head, maintaining eye contact.

"I'll wait out here," he finally said but didn't move.

A few seconds later, Will took a step back and let go of her waist.

She gripped the doorjamb for support and then stepped inside the bathroom. Will followed but only to place her change of clothes on the counter.

"If you need anything, I'm right here." He stepped out and, in a show of trust, closed the door behind him.

Memories of a younger Kelly struck him. Her freckle-cheeked smile. The way the sun bounced off her long hair. The easy way she'd laughed.

Even as kids he knew she came from the other side of town. Hell if he'd cared. The two got along and were fast friends. He remembered having a crush on her, his first real crush now that he thought back. The two had been inseparable at school. Her father would wait at the door some days. Will remembered the man had permanent worry lines creasing his face.

The difference in their economic status had never bothered Will. Looking back, it might've been a problem for Kelly and could explain why she'd always insisted on walking home by herself. He could walk her to the corner, but where the road forked and he turned left to go down the road to the ranch, she wouldn't allow him to walk with her. She forked right and to a side of town Will had never seen at age ten.

There were times she missed school. At first, he'd figured she was sick. She'd been out often, he'd noticed. She never wanted to talk about it and the subject dropped as soon as it came up.

What did he know as s kid?

The Kents had never known what it was like to miss a meal.

Looking back, Kelly must've. He'd noticed how little there'd been in her lunches at the cafeteria. When he'd asked she'd make up an excuse about not liking to eat a big lunch. She'd said it made her stomach cramp to eat too much before recess. How stupid he'd been not to realize she was covering. She'd been too proud to take anything from his plate. His lunches were packed to the brim with more fresh food than he had time to eat. Never one to waste, and being from a family that looked at wastefulness with the same vigor some people went to church, he'd brought home his leftovers and then had them for a snack after school. That came especially in handy when he'd joined athletics. He'd had almost a second full meal to chew on before hours-long practices began.

Kelly opened the door and held out the evidence bag.

She'd kicked off her boots and had tucked them under her other arm.

"Clothes look like they fit okay." He skimmed her body. Amber's T-shirt was tighter on Kelly and revealed a figure of generous curves and ample breasts. She stood there in her stocking feet, looking more lost and alone than he'd ever seen her, and he had to suppress the urge to pull her against his chest and be her comfort. An annoying voice reminded him that she wasn't his to comfort.

Dozens of questions flooded his mind. He didn't see a wedding ring and wanted to believe her that she wasn't the one who was supposed to get married.

"They'll do all right," she said and that honey-laced voice stirred other places he didn't want to acknowledge.

"Thanks for letting me shut the door," she said.

He tipped his chin before helping her down the hallway. She looked good in casual clothes with her hair tied away from her face.

"We'll need to head over to the hospital before my office," Zach said.

Will shot him a questioning look.

"Would you be more comfortable giving the rest of your statement to a female deputy?" Zach asked and the reason dawned on Will. Anger was an explosion in his chest.

"No. I'm fine. I already told you everything I can remember." She glanced from Zach to Will.

"Then let's go," Zach said.

The muscles on her face pulled taut.

"Mind if I tag along?" Will asked his cousin.

Before Zach could answer, Kelly said, "That would be great."

"Anyone I should call? Let them know that you'll be late today?" Will asked.

"There's no one special in my life right now and my cousin…" She wiped the moisture from her eyes.

The drive to the hospital took half an hour. Will had made a few calls using Bluetooth technology in his custom-made crossover vehicle so that everything would be expedited when she arrived.

He followed his cousin's SUV, respecting the fact that Kelly had to ride with him instead of Will. Protocol needed to be followed and especially since she couldn't be ruled out as a suspect. At this point, Zach was treating her like a witness, but that could change.

Zach pulled into the ER bay. Will parked nearby.

The look in Kelly's eyes when he'd first caught up to her would stay with him until he saw this thing through.

More memories stirred. He thought about the time she'd been cornered by Butch Dryden. Butch was tall and played sports. He'd filled out early, while Will was all height and gangly limbs. Butch stopped growing just shy of six feet tall. Will had shot past him by junior year of high school. Middle school was the time Butch had peaked.

Kelly had been beautiful even back then. Her shy smile wasn't easy to see or coax out of her. But it brightened her face when it finally made an appearance.

Butch had set his sights on Kelly becoming his

girlfriend. Much to Will's relief, she'd had no interest. At five feet eight inches by the fifth grade, one-hundred-sixty-pound Butch had become accustomed to taking what pleased him. That cold winter day in late February it had been Kelly.

Will had rounded the corner of the building after school that day. He'd had to stay late because the science teacher, Mrs. Pander, had asked if he could help her to her car with a prop she'd brought to class to illustrate the solar system. The 3-D model had to be broken down and taken to her SUV in pieces.

His helping Mrs. Pander saved Kelly from Butch, who had decided to pin her up against the wall and force her to kiss him while he touched her.

Kelly might've been shy but she knew how to stand up for herself. As Will had rounded the corner she'd belted Butch, blackening his eye.

Will chuckled at the memory of her jerking back her fist, her face wrinkled with pain from hitting such a hard skull.

What had come next wasn't so funny.

Will had stepped in and, after getting in a couple of good swings, took a decent beating. It was the last fight Will had lost. Unless he counted his relationship with Lacey. That had been a KO.

That same fighting spirit in Kelly's eyes had returned earlier. But if he looked too deep, he also saw pain and loss.

He chalked up his offer to see this through to old protective instincts kicking in. He should know when to leave something alone. When to walk away. He put the gearshift in Park and leaned both elbows against his steering wheel.

It was the middle of the night and he'd need to get up in a couple of hours to work the cattle ranch. Speaking of which, they needed to be informed of what had happened on the property. He'd wait until sunrise to give them updates. Kelly was all right. That was the only thing that mattered right now.

So when his cell buzzed in his pocket he was caught off guard.

Will glanced at the screen. It was Mitch, the oldest brother and the only one older than Will.

"What's going on?" Will asked. "Why are you up so late?"

"I just put the twins down for the second time tonight and saw your text about following Kelly to the hospital."

"What are they doing awake at this hour?" he asked, watching in the rearview as an expensive-looking custom-model sports car parked in the ambulance bay.

From this distance, Will saw the silhouette of a medium-size, slightly build man climb out of the sporty red vehicle. He rushed past the turnstile and disappeared.

"Stuffy noses. Rea had a fever so it's only a matter of time before Aaron does." No matter how tired Mitch sounded Will knew that his brother wouldn't trade his life with his kids for the world. He was the happiest Will had ever seen him. All of which had to do with the happiness he had when his wife had returned. Kimberly had been forced to fake her death in order to disappear from men who were hunting her because her foster father—the man who'd adopted her—was murdered. Her father had helped out a desperate young man and put himself in the sights of a deadly human-trafficking ring. Mitch and Kimberly had been through hell and back, but had come out the stronger for it.

"Tell me what's going on with Kelly."

"What do you remember about her family?" Will asked.

"Not much. Seems like her parents blew into town. Her father made a lot of people mad and then he picked up the family in the middle of the night and left. Only reason I remember any of it is because Mrs. Owen complained for years to Mom about him leaving town without paying anyone back, including her. Put a few people in a rough spot for a while, according to her."

"I don't remember her mother much. Do you?" Will asked, hoping his older brother's memory was more reliable than his own.

"She did hair for some folks. That's about all I know," Mitch admitted. "Why?"

"Just curious."

"The two of you were tight at one time. You don't recall anything about her family?" Mitch asked.

"Not really. I was too young back then to remember my homework let alone what went on in town."

"Pop kept us busy on the ranch." Mitch chuckled.

There was always work to be done and William

Kent had always included his children in the family business. Patricia, their mother, had always insisted on allowing them to be children with plenty of playtime. Pop would wink at her when she voiced her concerns about her children growing up too fast. He'd knock off work early and take them into town for ice cream or to a movie the next day just to show her that he hadn't forgotten kids needed to have fun. Pop had joked that it had taken having a second son to convince his wife to name a child after him.

Of course, growing up on a ranch with land as far as the eye could see, animals everywhere and a big family with his cousins, Zach and Amy, over every day had been a magical childhood as far as Will was concerned. There'd been eight kids running around, not including those of the ranch boss, Jessup. His added another four to the mix and Will's mother had called them a dozen angels. She might've come up with another name if she'd known what they were really up to half the time. They were all good kids, don't get him wrong. Thinking back, they'd been a handful with all the antics to go along with it.

But Will had become restless in his teenage years after his girlfriend became sick. She'd moved to Chicago to be closer to a specialist there and Will had lost touch with her after. He'd never been one for social media or he guessed they could've kept in touch. Now that his mother and father were gone his losses were piling up.

Instead of going to college like everyone else, he'd joined the military, needing to find his own definition of what it meant to be a man. He was proud of serving his country even though it had cost him a relationship with the woman he believed he was going to spend the rest of his life with, Lacey.

Stay down the mental road trip he was on and he'd find the expressway to pain and suffering. So, he shoved aside those thoughts and snapped back to the present, to his phone call with Mitch.

"Kelly's cousin has been reported missing. I'll get a picture to circulate in case she turns up on the ranch," Will said.

"We can do better than that. I'll alert the men and we'll formulate a search party," Mitch offered.

"Her vehicle was found near the Jasper property. I doubt we'll find Christina on the ranch but it never hurts to be aware," Will stated. "Everyone needs to be on full alert considering the shooter might be on the ranch somewhere, looking for Kelly. Zach will have deputies out today in order to gather more evidence. He likely already got shell casings collected in order to send over to forensics for analysis."

"Maybe we'll get lucky and find a match," Mitch stated.

"What about Kelly?" Mitch asked. "What's next for her?"

"She doesn't remember much. Says she was forced to drink something and the description of the man she gave doesn't match up to the shooter," Will told him.

"That sounds like something out of a crime show."

"It's weird," Will agreed. "I'd like to speak to

the man who was supposed to perform the wedding ceremony."

"You think she's lying?"

"She believes what she's saying," Will said. The clock read 2:48 a.m. "I'd better head inside and check on her. She's been through a lot. I don't want her to be alone right now."

"Be careful," Mitch warned. "I know how you are when someone needs your help. You go all in. I feel the need to remind you of the fact she had on a wedding dress."

"I'm aware." Will thanked his brother for his concern. "I'm also not going to walk away from a case that involves me being shot at on our property. I don't have to remind you of the anniversary that just passed."

"Nope. It's all I've been thinking about all month," Mitch admitted. Of course, his brother would be concerned about everyone's safety. He had always taken on a protective role within the family and the business.

"The MO is completely different and I doubt what happened with Kelly has anything to do with the event a few days ago, but I have every intention of finding out." Will's defenses were a little too high when it came to Kelly.

This wasn't the time to examine his out-of-place reaction to seeing her again.

There was something sticking in his craw and he needed to go in there and figure out what it was.

Chapter Six

The twin towers of Mercy General were a stark white against the canopy of black sky. An almost all-glass atrium-style lobby sat in between. Will walked inside, his boots clicking on the oversize shiny white tiles.

"Kelly Morgan's room, please," he said to the attendant with a name tag that read Esther.

"I'll check for you. Just a moment," Esther said. She performed a double take. "Are you one of the Kent boys?"

He nodded even though he'd long since grown into a man.

"I know it's been a couple of years but it's such a shame about your father," Esther said. "He was such a good man and even after all this time is still missed."

Will thanked her for her kindness. William Kent had left behind big boots to fill. That was for damn sure.

Esther focused on the small screen in front of

her and punched a few computer keys, hunt-and-peck style.

Sweet as the older woman was, at this rate Kelly would be discharged before Will found out her room number.

Time ticked by and Will tried his level best not to tap the toe of his boot impatiently.

Esther's forehead wrinkled as she studied the screen like it was a heart-rate monitor and a life depended on her noticing any dip in status.

Will took in a slow breath, reminding himself of one of his mother's favorite quotes—*patience is bitter but its fruit is sweet.* He had the bitter part down, he thought wryly.

"Hold on. Now, it must be here somewhere," Esther said. She really looked to be trying to her hardest to find the information. Peck. Peck. Peck. Squint. Peck. Peck. Peck. Squint.

"She would've been admitted—" he checked his watch "—ten to fifteen minutes ago."

Esther glanced up and wagged her finger at him. "You should've told me that sooner. That's a different story. Do you know which tower?"

"That one." He pointed to the east.

"Ah. Okay. Now we're getting somewhere." Esther picked up the phone and pushed a button. She glanced down at the desk, tapping a long painted fingernail on the pile of papers in front of her. "Do you have a new patient?… Uh-huh. Yes. That's right. Last name is Morgan," she said into the receiver as she rocked her head.

She ended the call and looked up at Will. "East tower, fourth level. There's a waiting room. Someone will be at the check-in desk."

"Thank you," Will said, turning and increasing his pace toward the bank of elevators on the east side of the lobby.

Will checked in with the attendant—Margaret—who asked him to take a seat while she spoke to the doctor.

"I'll stand," he said.

He paced.

The blue chairs were nestled in rows. Will stalked toward the floor-to-ceiling window. All he could see was a reflection of the room until he got so close to the glass that he'd bang his nose if he took another step.

His truck sat underneath a streetlight and all he had was a view of the parking lot.

Another ten minutes of pacing and Will was about to go find the room for himself, but then Margaret returned.

"Sorry about the wait," she said. "She's in room 432."

Will thanked Margaret on his way out the door. He hooked an immediate left and followed the signs until he stood in front of 432.

The door was half-open so he slipped inside.

A man kneeled beside her bed. Will immediately assumed the medium-height and slight man was Fletcher Hardaway.

The successful Fort Worth entrepreneur wore

expensive-looking jogging pants, the kind that had never seen a hard workout or a gym, a cotton shirt and a designer watch.

Kelly glanced up at Will the minute he entered with a pleading look in her eyes. Hardaway didn't seem to notice.

"Why wait?" he asked, continuing on with his conversation—a conversation that seemed to be making Kelly uncomfortable based on the tension lines written across her forehead.

Seeing her eased an uncomfortable ache in Will's chest. More information he didn't need to examine.

"I—" she began but was cut off.

"The wedding itself isn't important. How it happens is no longer an issue. I want you to be my wife, Kelly," Hardaway said. "What exactly would we be holding off for?"

"That's not what I remember." Kelly's tone left no room for argument. "We broke up."

"I'm sorry this happened and threw a wrench in our plans. I still want to marry you and there's no reason to wait. I called Howard Bell on the way over," he continued, running like a steam engine over her refutation.

She balked. "The justice of the peace?"

"He said he'd open the courthouse tonight. We can still get married today just like we'd planned."

What was the rush?

"Technically, it's tomorrow," Will stated, his arms folded across his chest.

Hardaway whirled around on Will.

A strange unfamiliar feeling came over Will—odd, because jealousy was out of place. He had no designs on Kelly. Sure, they'd been childhood friends and he could admit that she'd probably been his first real crush, but that was years ago. He chalked up his current feelings to nostalgia as he introduced himself to the Fort Worth millionaire.

Hardaway didn't stand, but took the outstretched hand Will offered. The man's handshake was soft and his palms were sweaty.

Tension sat in the room, thick as a heavy fog.

"Will saved my life," Kelly blurted out and he figured she was trying to fill the awkward silence that followed the goodwill gesture.

"Then I owe you," Hardaway said, tipping his face toward Will. The man's smile, a show of perfect straight teeth, and his words had a forced quality to them.

For someone whose fiancée had gone missing and been chased by a gunman on their wedding day, he didn't seem as upset as Will would've expected. In fact, as he sized up the guy, Will couldn't help but wonder why he wasn't still in his tux.

"Thank you for stopping by to check on my fiancée." Hardaway emphasized those last two words a little intensely to Will's thinking.

Will leaned against the wall near the door. He had no plans to leave. He'd pitch a tent if he had one just to see the man's reaction.

The move didn't seem to sit well with Hardaway, but Will wasn't going anywhere. An attempt had been made on Kelly's life. Someone had shot at both of them.

Her fiancé wasn't there to stop it, but his biggest worry seemed to be getting her to the altar.

"What's the rush on the wedding plans?" Will asked.

"I've been sick with worry," Hardaway said, refocusing on Kelly. His words were dramatic, if not his actions.

Will decided not to point out the fact that the man had taken time to shower and change clothes. Were those really the actions of a man half out of his mind with worry? They could be the actions of a man who knew exactly what was going to happen next. Or, at least, thought he did.

The worst part of this whole scenario was how lost and alone Kelly looked. It was a sucker punch to Will's gut to see her like that.

A knock sounded at the door.

"Come in," Kelly said quickly.

Zach walked in and Will appreciated the break in tension.

"Mind if we talk in the hall?" Zach asked Hardaway after acknowledging Will.

Hardaway stood and glanced nervously at Kelly, then asked, "Will you be all right, darling?"

The word stuck in Will's craw. Worse yet, the sappy sweetness of it all. Why didn't the man save all that syrup for Sunday-morning pancakes?

"I'm good," Kelly quipped.

The minute Hardaway disappeared, Kelly motioned for Will to sit on the bed next to her. He did, but couldn't say he was especially comfortable being alone in a room with another man's fiancée. There were some lines that couldn't be crossed even though she denied any marital ties to Hardaway.

"There's something about him that scares me," she said to Will. He didn't like the idea she would be afraid of any man and especially not one she was supposed to marry if Hardaway could be believed. Will's gut instinct told him the man was lying, but Kelly's memory couldn't be relied upon if the drugged story panned out and he had no reason to doubt her. Dr. Carter had said that her memory should come back. It could be in pieces or all at once. He hadn't found any blunt-force trauma to her head during his examination, so the only explanation for her memory lapse was the drug.

"Does he seem like he's acting right to you?" she asked.

"Honestly, no."

"He wants to take me to his house. He keeps calling it our new home but nothing about what he's saying rings true to me," she admitted.

"Has he been physical with you in the past?" he asked outright.

She stared at him blankly. "There's no way I'd stay with anyone who hit me, if that's what you're asking."

"You had no plans to stay with him. Remember?"

"I don't really. All I know is that he makes me

feel scared and I have no business being in a wedding dress," she responded.

"And yet the dress fit you. I know from my sister's friends that wedding dresses have to be tailored," he said.

She bit her bottom lip. "You have a point."

And then her eyes studied him. "There's nothing about that man I find attractive anymore. I know we dated in the past, a while ago. But I feel nothing but fear when he's close by. Don't you think that's strange?"

"I do." He looked her square in the eye. "But what do you want me to do, Kelly? You show up on my property in a wedding dress saying you can't remember why you're wearing it. There's blood on your dress and you're cut up. Before I can get anything out of you, someone chases us with a shotgun. And now your cousin goes missing and meanwhile your fiancé shows up looking like he knew what was about to happen."

"Exactly," she said, like he'd just outlined all her points perfectly.

"I don't like him," Will admitted. "But it might not be for reasons you think."

"You want to explain?" Her eyebrows knitted together.

"Not really." Will didn't want to admit to her—hell, to himself—that old feelings seemed to be seeping in and were making it impossible for him to be objective. Mitch had been quick to point it out, though.

She made eyes at him like she was urging him to talk.

When his mouth remained clamped shut, she said, “He wants me to go home with him and it creeps me out. Something feels off when he’s in the room. It’s like I can’t breathe and I’m scared to speak my mind.”

“Did he ever do anything to physically hurt you?” Will asked.

“No. I don’t remember anything like that. I just have a horrible feeling anytime he comes near me, and my skin crawls like a thousand fire ants are on me,” she stated. “I feel like I need to run far just to get away from him.”

“Is there any chance he’s the man wearing the tux you mentioned earlier?” Will had to ask because the shooter didn’t match Tux’s description.

“No. I don’t think so. Fletcher’s too small.”

The description was off to him, too, but it didn’t hurt to double check. Besides, whatever drug she’d been given may have altered her perceptions. Whatever it was might’ve distorted her vision and senses.

“The thing is, I’m afraid to go home alone to my place with my cousin missing and I know I’m not going anywhere with *him*,” she stated and he tried damn hard not to focus on the moisture gathering in her eyes. Or the way the corner of her mouth twitched when she mentioned Hardaway.

“Come to the ranch.” His siblings wouldn’t mind a guest for a few days until this could be sorted out. His logical mind said the invitation was a bad idea, but it was too late to take back the offer now. Besides, part of him needed to see for himself that she'd be all right and whoever had been bold enough to shoot at him on his family's property needed to be found and brought to justice. This whole scenario had been dumped on his doorstep and Will didn't like it.

"I couldn't." But the flicker of hope in her eyes said she could be swayed.

"You landed on my family's property, and in my book that means we're responsible for your safety. Until Zach can figure out who did the shooting, find your cousin and you can go home safely, it's the only choice that makes sense," he argued. "You need a safe place to rest. Those wounds aren't going to heal themselves without some tending to. Maybe your memory will come back once you've had a chance to rest. Plus, it'll give him time to cool off."

She didn't put up much of a fight.

The hope in her eyes put a chink in his armor and that was another reason he knew this was a bad idea.

"Only if you're sure I won't get in the way there," she finally said. "And only until we figure out where my cousin is." Her eyes brightened. "That's another thing. My cousin is my best friend. I would never get married without her there. So, where is she?"

Zach filled the door frame. Hardaway entered the room next, but at roughly five feet ten inches with a slight build, he looked more like Zach's shadow.

"Nurse said you could leave as long as I promised to make sure you get plenty of rest. Let's get you dressed and packed up," Hardaway said to her. Will noticed a sense of urgency in the man's tone that shot another warning flare in the sky.

"Good. Everything hurts and I really need a shower," she said, pushing up to sit. Movement looked like it hurt and Will figured the physical aches were minor compared to the emotional trauma she'd endured.

Hardaway made a move toward her but Will stepped in between them in order to block his path.

A look of shock crossed Hardaway's features. Up close, the man had bags underneath dishonest-looking blue eyes. They were too blue. Sure, Hardaway had that sandy-hair, blue-eye thing going that Will guessed some women could find attractive. The man didn't seem Kelly's type at all, but that was none of Will's business.

"You can go home now, Fletcher," Kelly said.

Hardaway thumped Will's chest, which had Will instinctively rearing back to belt the man. Zach caught Will's elbow from the side.

"There's no reason to get excited," Zach said, trying to smooth over the situation.

Will wouldn't lose his temper and he had better sense than to belt a man like Hardaway without being cornered. Even with witnesses saying Hardaway started it, Will would look like the bad guy if he swung first like he'd been about to. He appreciated Zach's intervention.

"Darling, you're coming home with me." Hardaway's chest was puffed up like a silverback gorilla in a fight for territory.

"I don't need a ride," Kelly said to him, "so just leave."

"It's silly for you to pay for a car when mine's downstairs and we're going to the same place." Hardaway's glare would be intimidating to most women.

"I already asked Will for a ride," Kelly said to him in no uncertain terms. "So, just go home."

Hardaway looked ready to buck up for a fight. "I'm not leaving here without you, Kelly."

There was so much underlying threat in those words. Will felt himself tense up again. If Hardaway was looking for a fight, Will had no intention of shying away, lawyers or not.

"I mean it. I'm not going to your house." Kelly emphasized those last two words. "Last time I checked I still live alone and, besides, it's none of your business where I go when I'm released. I can take care of myself."

In an athletic stance with his fists clenched, Hardaway looked ready to physically force her. His bravado lasted until Will said, "She'll walk out of this room with you when hell freezes over as long as I'm standing here."

And then Will saw something else in the man's eyes. It wasn't more than a flicker of panic. Will was glad Hardaway got the message.

"The woman stated her intention. Now, it's time for you to realize when you've lost a fight and head back where you came from." Will didn't need to fist his hands or clench his back teeth for Hardaway to realize he was barking up the wrong tree.

One look was all that was necessary.

The Fort Worth magnate's body language was pretty damn clear to Will. He didn't want a fight with someone his equal.

"Instead of making this worse, why don't you go home and calm down," Zach interjected, stepping in between the businessman and Will.

Hardaway blew out a sharp breath. "You're making a big mistake, Kelly."

"She has a good handle on what she's comfortable doing," Will stated.

"You are, too. Do you have any idea what family you're dealing with?" When the magnate got no reaction from either one of them, he turned and then stalked out the door, mumbling something about suing the sheriff's office. The man's nerves seemed to be strung so tight they might snap. Will would put money on the fact that Hardaway was up to something.

But what?

Murder?

No good could come out of forcing a woman to marry him. Will had taken the hint when Lacey had left him at the aisle. She'd come back a week later, crying and saying she'd made a mistake. Will had heard her out. The only mistake that had happened, in his estimation, was that he'd believed that she'd loved him in the first place.

"I'm really sorry about that, about him," Kelly said to Will.

"It's not your fault," Will stated.

She flashed eyes at him that said she believed otherwise.

"I know what he's saying but none of this feels right to me, Will." She picked up her folded clothes from the bedside table.

Her eyes were red and her shoulders rounded. Exhaustion looked to be overtaking her. She needed rest and probably a good meal.

"We'll get to the bottom of whatever's going on," Will promised. "Zach's the best at what he does and he'll find your cousin. I'll stick around until you get your memory back."

He decided to pass on pointing out that she might actually *want* to marry Hardaway when her memory returned. Although, not one of her actions so far logically fit with that line of thinking.

"Ready?" he asked, because Zach stood at the doorway, and Will was certain that his cousin was assessing Will's mental condition.

"Almost. I just need to get dressed." She excused herself to the bathroom as he walked over to the window.

"How long have you known her?" Zach asked quietly.

"We go far back," Will said.

"You ought to considering the fact you're bringing her home to the ranch with you," Zach stated as Will looked out the window.

Hardaway stood in the parking lot, his hip leaned against his car, and he looked to be having a rather intense conversation on his cell phone.

"You should come take a look at this," Will said to Zach, grateful for the chance to turn the attention away from him and toward the person Zach really needed to watch carefully—Fletcher Hardaway.

Zach walked over, stopping just short of standing beside Will.

"Look at that." Will motioned toward the man whose free arm was flailing wildly around in heated conversation.

A buzzing noise broke into the moment.

Zach checked his phone. "It's a text." He glanced up at Will and one look said this situation was about to go from bad to worse.

"The blood type splattered inside the victim's vehicle matches that of what was found on the wedding dress," he stated.

"So you're saying they're a match," Will clarified.

Zach took in a sharp breath. "Neither of which are a match to the witness's blood type."

"You know she's not involved like that. It makes no sense that she would disappear from her own wedding, make up a story about a man in a tux, go for a car ride with her cousin and then…what? Try to hurt her?" He didn't say "kill" her but the implication sat thickly in the air. "Oh, and just to make things interesting she took off and was being chased by a man with a gun who then tried to shoot both of us? Come on, Zach. Who was the shooter? And what was he doing chasing her onto my family's ranch?"

"Those aren't my words but you've highlighted a lot of issues that need to be resolved," Zach said.

"Are you saying that I'm a suspect?" Kelly asked point-blank, emerging from the bathroom with a stunned expression on her face. Her violet eyes were wide and her fists were planted on her hips.

"No. But I am saying you're an important witness," Zach stated.

"She's innocent," Will demanded, his tone rising defensively.

"I never said that she wasn't," Zach admitted. "But right now I have a woman missing who is tied to Kelly. There's blood spatter in a car and on her wedding dress for a wedding she doesn't even remember agreeing to be part of, and is an exact match. Logic says the blood spatter is a match to the victim, but we have no idea where Ms. Foxwood is so we can't test out the theory. Evidence points to the fact that Kelly was inside the vehicle."

Spelled out like that, Will could see the problems. Most of the evidence so far pointed to Kelly.

Chapter Seven

The drive home from the hospital took less than an hour. Exhaustion made Kelly's arms feel like they had hundred-pound weights attached to them.

"You also have a jealous fiancé—" Before Will could finish Kelly flashed eyes at him. Fletcher Hardaway was most definitely not the love of her life. She knew that on a soul-deep level.

"Can we stop calling him that? At least for now? I've already been clear on that point, Will. I'm not engaged or getting married to Fletcher Hardaway."

Will helped her out of his vehicle and into the house from the garage.

"Then we'll call him a businessman," Will stated. "One whose mental stability is in question in my book."

Kelly leaned her weight against Will, ignoring the chemistry pinging between them where their hips made contact. Will had grown into the kind of man who'd leave a trail of broken hearts in his wake.

"Your house is beautiful," Kelly said to Will as he flipped on a light and helped her into the living room. Twin brown leather sofas faced each other in front of a large tumbled stone fireplace. The living room was open to an eating area and large kitchen. High cathedral ceilings, with a wooden beam running along the top, gave a sense of space.

When she really looked around, she noticed that nothing was out of place. Glancing around with the light on, she also couldn't help but realize the place was immaculate. No dirty dishes in the sink or plates on the counter. No stacks of mail anywhere to be seen.

On second look, the place was a little too perfect, too orderly for someone to actually live there.

"Is this your home?"

"Technically, the place belongs to me. I've been waiting for the right time to move in officially." A hint of emotion crossed behind his eyes that resembled a storm brewing.

"Waiting for what? It's beautiful here."

He shrugged noncommittally and she recalled reading about his father's passing.

"I'm sorry about your dad," she said. "He was a good man."

Will thanked her but the storm intensified behind his eyes and she figured she'd struck a nerve. The intensity of his gaze gave her the feeling she should back away from the subject. Were his feelings still raw?

Kelly knew exactly what it was like to lose people she loved too soon.

"What about your family?" Will turned the tables.

It was Kelly's turn to shrug, the pain still too fresh to talk about even all these years after losing her baby brother and father.

"There's coffee but other than that the kitchen is missing a few supplies. I'll run out in the morning for food." Will seemed to pick up on her mood and she was grateful for the change in subject.

"I don't want to be any trouble," she stated but he waved her off.

"You'd do the same if the situation was reversed," he said.

"How do you know?" There was no doubt that she would, but she was curious to find out where his confidence in her came from.

"You always gave a pencil to anyone even if it was your last and you had to use a pen." That storm brewed again. "Some things don't change about a person."

The words sat between them.

"He's not my fiancé," she said, capitalizing on the sentiment. "I know that I can't prove it but that doesn't mean I'm any less certain."

"Give it a few days. Your memory will come back. We'll get to the bottom of what's going on." With his arm around her waist and the strong, masculine Will beside her, she couldn't think clearly much beyond right now. The strange need to defend herself against the notion she was about to marry a man like Fletcher struck her as odd. She'd made her case a couple of times already. It was time to let it go and move on.

This close, Will's musky aftershave filled her

senses with every intake of breath. He smelled clean and spicy.

"What if Christina is trying to reach me on my cell?" she asked. "I didn't think about it before but she would try to contact me if she was in trouble. I know she'd try to reach me if there was any way possible."

The thought of anything happening to her cousin knocked air from her lungs. She stumbled, still exhausted, and Will tightened his grip around her.

"Zach will find her by morning."

She noticed that he didn't say "alive." Will had always been honest and never made promises he couldn't keep, not even in grade school.

"He's good at his job and his deputies will keep working until she turns up."

"Maybe I should reach out to her. Try to call her cell." Kelly bit back a curse. "I actually can't remember the last time I memorized someone's phone number. If she's out there alone she could be hurt or disoriented."

She struggled to contain a yawn and lost.

"Your eyes are about to close while you're standing up, which you can't do without my help." He made good points. "There's not much else you can do tonight. You'll think more clearly with a few hours of shut-eye."

She glanced down at the bloodstains on her forearm. The nurse had wiped most of it off for her after the exam, but some was still caked on her skin. "Mind if I borrow your shower?"

The storm behind his eyes picked up steam and it was like rolling gray clouds behind his eyes. "Go ahead."

"And… Will?"

"Yeah."

"Would you stand outside the door and wait for me?" Kelly hated the feeling of being afraid. But she was still in the grips of whatever that drug she'd been given was—ketamine was the doctor's best guess. Her mouth had been swabbed and it was dry as cotton now, but they wouldn't know lab results for a few days at the earliest.

And right now, she was scared.

A NOISE SOUNDED in the next room, jolting Kelly from a deep sleep. She must've gasped as she shot straight up to a sitting position.

"I'm right here. You're okay." Will's voice grounded her. That deep timbre soothed her more than she knew better to allow. *Complicated* didn't begin to describe her life.

Kelly pulled up the covers to her chin, suddenly aware of the fact that the only thing she had on was one of his old T-shirts.

A chuckle rumbled up and out of his chest, filling the space with its vibration. "There's a robe at the foot of the bed. I'll answer the door while you put it on."

He'd been sitting in an armchair across the room. She remembered asking him to wait for her while she showered and then if he'd stay in her room just until she fell asleep.

Had he slept in that uncomfortable chair all night?

The clock on the nightstand said she hadn't been out much more than a couple of hours and her body felt every bit of the lack of REM. Everything was sore. Movement hurt. Her head felt like it might burst. She hurt physically and emotionally.

"Any word on Christina?" she immediately asked.

"I'm sorry." He held up his phone and shook his head.

She tightened her grip on the covers, ever more aware of wearing only a T-shirt with his masculine presence in the room.

Will stood and took the couple of steps toward the door. "Don't worry, Kelly. I didn't see anything for you to be embarrassed about."

He closed the door and she exhaled, not realizing she'd been holding her breath.

Kelly checked to make the blanket had been covering her before she grabbed the white cotton bathrobe at the foot of the bed. She slipped it on and threw her feet over the side of the bed.

Movement made her nauseous. She doubled over and gripped her stomach, which was churning.

There was a bottle of water next to the bed. She snapped it up and removed the lid. Her mouth was drier than Texas soil in a drought. Gulping the clear liquid brought a shiver as she remembered the last time someone was trying to force a drink down her throat.

Her thoughts immediately focused on Christina. Her cousin was several years older than Kelly and had literally saved her life. She'd given her refuge when Kelly's life had become one catastrophic storm after the next.

Kelly silently prayed that her cousin was home, sleeping. But a niggling feeling in the back of her mind said something was very wrong. She'd feel better when she spoke to Christina, which wouldn't happen sitting in Will Kent's guest bedroom. He'd tried to get her to take the master last night, but there was no way she could let that happen.

She glanced at the chair and wondered if he'd gotten any sleep. Her mind was bouncing around in all directions and she still felt a little disoriented. The nurse had told her to expect it.

A female's voice in the next room shot an inappropriate pang of jealousy through her. She hadn't seen a ring on Will's finger but that didn't mean he was single. She'd just assumed because there were no feminine touches around his house, but then in his own words he hadn't moved into the place yet.

In everything that had happened last night, she hadn't thought to ask if someone would miss him coming home to wherever he actually lived. Was it with the woman in the next room?

Kelly's thoughts quickly wound back to Christina. She forced herself up and into the bathroom. She washed her face and was grateful to see a new toothbrush and a tube of toothpaste on the vanity. There was a brush and some hair bands. Again, jealousy jabbed harder than a prizefighter. A man wouldn't likely think to have these supplies on hand in a guest bathroom.

Kelly pushed aside those unproductive thoughts, realizing that she felt more of a pull toward Will than the man claiming to be her fiancé.

She stepped into the hallway, took a fortifying breath and walked into the living area.

The woman in the kitchen looked familiar but Kelly couldn't place her. That green-eyed monster called jealousy was playing havoc with her emotions. She told herself she felt this way toward Will because he'd saved her life. The fact that they had a history only intensified those feelings.

Will hugged the woman and thanked her for doing his shopping.

From the back, the mystery woman was short-ish and had a long mane of thick, wavy hair. She had a cute figure—something else that Kelly didn't want to notice.

"Do you need help walking?" Will's focus shifted and he stepped away from the mystery woman, who spun around.

"Amy McWilliams?" Kelly asked, realizing why the woman seemed so familiar. She was Will's younger cousin, Zach's sister. Kelly remembered her from after school. Amy had been much younger.

Relief she had no right to own washed over her. If Will was in a relationship, Kelly didn't need to know about it.

Amy smiled her greeting.

"I wasn't sure what you liked to eat for breakfast so I brought a little of everything," Amy said. Her bright, bubbly personality was the same as Kelly remembered from school, only she was older and more mature with a smile on her face and a twinkle in her eyes that hinted at mischief. "There's fresh fruit, yogurt, pastries and cereal."

"I'll get a pot of coffee on," Will stated. "Come sit down." He motioned toward the bar chairs surrounding the granite island that separated the kitchen from the eating space before getting to work on that coffee.

"My brother called." Amy stocked the fridge. "Said I should tell you that he's on his way."

"Did he say why?" Will asked.

"All he said was that it's important and he wanted to be the one to tell you." Amy shrugged. "I have no idea what it's about."

"When do you head back to school?" Will asked.

"Sunday night," she said.

It was nice to talk about something normal for a change instead of the doom and gloom that felt like it was always nearby, ready to smother Kelly. She could see how much Will cared about his cousin. The only person in the world Kelly had felt a bond like that with was her cousin, Christina.

"What are you doing home, anyway? Aren't final exams coming up?" Will asked.

Amy spun around to face him. "Mom?"

She burst out laughing at her own joke.

Kelly couldn't help herself. She laughed, too. "His hair is rather short for the job."

"What's wrong with my hair?" Will asked and then he allowed himself a small smile.

"Exactly," Amy said. She turned to Kelly. "Speaking of being mothered, what sounds good to eat?"

"Maybe yogurt would go down okay," Kelly said, "but I can get it for myself."

Amy was already waving off Kelly with one hand and opening the fridge with the other. "I'm right here. It's no trouble."

The coffeemaker finished with a beep.

"How many cups am I pouring?" Will asked.

"None for me," Amy said quickly. "I can't stay."

"Two it is," Will stated as Amy handed over a spoon to Kelly.

"Thank you," Kelly said.

"Not a problem," Amy said with a sweet smile. "I better get on my way. I need to stop in and check on a friend before getting back on I-35." The word *friend* had a little too much emphasis and Kelly immediately picked up on the fact that it was most likely a guy.

Will seemed to catch it, as well, based on his hiked eyebrow. So, Kelly diverted attention. "I take it you're at UT Austin."

"Junior year." Amy nodded. "Graduation can't get here soon enough."

"Be careful on the highway today," Will warned. "There's a big game this weekend in Waco."

"Gr-r-reat." Amy rolled her eyes. "Just what I need. An eight-hour drive that should take less than half that long."

She smacked her hand on the granite and then shrugged. “What are you gonna do?”

The yogurt was going down surprisingly well.

“You sure you don’t want a to-go cup of coffee for the road?” Will asked.

“Nah. I’m good.” Amy looked to Kelly as she scooped her car keys off the granite countertop. “And you guys be careful around here. Scary what happened yesterday.”

“The security team’s been alerted,” Will said after taking a sip of fresh brew.

Kelly stared at her coffee mug as reality slammed into her.

“Fletcher Hardaway is all over the internet this morning,” Amy said, holding up her cell. She made sympathetic eyes at Kelly.

“What’s that about?” Will asked. He’d been casually leaning one hip against the counter. He had on jeans and no shirt and Kelly forced her eyes away from his strong male form.

“He’s offering a huge reward to anyone who has information about Christina Foxwood’s whereabouts or leading to the arrest of the man who tried to shoot his fiancée. He mentioned something about a man wearing a tuxedo.”

Will cursed and it was exactly the same word Kelly was thinking.

“Why would he do that?” Kelly wanted her cousin back safely but Fletcher should’ve cleared this with her before sending out a message to the world. But then she wondered if he had ulterior motives.

"Whatever his reasoning he just made the investigation that much harder." Will cursed again.

"Think that's what Zach is coming over to talk about?" Kelly asked.

"Nah. I got the impression he has some other kind of news," Amy said. She looked intensely at Will for a second. "Keep your eyes open around here. Okay?"

Will pulled her in for a hug. The younger cousin looked so small in comparison.

And then Amy walked straight over to Kelly, keys jingling with each step. "You, too. Be careful. Hope to see you around again."

After a warm embrace, Amy excused herself and bounded toward the door.

As she opened it, her brother was standing there with a raised fist. His look of surprise said he was about to knock.

Both siblings were startled. A quick hug followed a greeting and more warnings to be safe all around.

Zach stepped inside, looking like he hadn't slept.

"You're not going to like this," he warned.

Chapter Eight

Will noticed Kelly's white-knuckle grip around her coffee mug. He offered to freshen his cousin's coffee, which he'd walked in with. After pouring, Zach got down to business.

"Amy told us about what Fletcher pulled," Kelly began, clearly embarrassed by the man who was supposed to be her fiancé. "I'm sorry you're having to deal with that."

"He's made a mess of things at my office," Zach admitted. "Phones are ringing nonstop and I don't have the staff to field the calls. We put a call out for volunteers in hopes we can train them to take down information and vet out possible leads for our deputies. The gunman is still at large."

Kelly flinched. It was easy to see that she blamed herself.

"Those aren't the reasons that I'm here. This visit has to do with the ranch." Will didn't like the sound of his cousin's voice one bit.

He leaned his hip against the counter and took a sip of coffee, waiting for the bomb to drop.

"I had a meeting with some of your brothers and sister at the main house earlier this morning and I wanted to stop by to tell you personally what's going on. While searching for the gunman on your property yesterday, one of my deputies found another butchered heifer," Zach stated.

"Like the one from the other day?" Will asked, noticing Kelly's furrowed brow.

"That's right. I already called Hank Porter out to take a look and see if he can estimate a timeline for when it happened," Zach said. "All I can say so far is that it's been more than a couple of days."

Dr. Porter, best known to the Kent family and friends as Hank, was the best big-animal vet in the state.

Will released a string of curse words under his breath. He raked his fingers through his thick hair. "What the hell is going on?"

Will looked at a confused Kelly, who, by the way, had managed to make a white cotton robe look sexy. The thought was inappropriate under the circumstances, so he pushed it out of his mind. "A few days ago one of our heifers was found near Rushing Creek with a missing left hoof. She'd been butchered and left to die."

Kelly drew back like she'd been slapped. "That poor thing. To know that she suffered must be tearing you apart. I know how much you and your family have always cared about your animals."

Will shouldn't be shocked that she knew him. The two of them did have a history that went way back and he'd always been kind to animals. It was in his DNA. And yet her words struck a chord with him, anyway. It was nice to be around someone who really knew him but didn't share DNA.

"I'm guessing there are no tracks and no prints in the area." Logic said this was the same person as before.

"Nothing yet. I'm hopeful we'll get something this go-round," Zach admitted.

Four days. A left hoof. A heifer. "What's the connection that we're missing?"

"We don't have much to go on," Zach said. "That's more than we had when this whole ordeal started last week."

"Also rules out random teenagers, doesn't it?" It had been wishful thinking at best to hold onto the hope this would be a one-time occurrence.

"Does in my book." Zach took a sip of coffee.

"The cult theory could hold true. There could be a ritual that takes place this time of year requiring an animal sacrifice," Will said, theorizing.

"Ellen's doing an internet search as we speak. She also called up the town librarian to get her on the job of researching cults who sacrifice animals in the month of December," he said, referring to his secretary. "I've reached out to every sheriff's office I'm familiar with across the state to let them know what's going on. We have no idea the true scope of what could be happening until we hear back from other offices. Of course, many folks might not report the crime and so I've asked other offices to educate their people on what's happening here. The more eyes and ears we get on this, the better."

It sounded like Zach was covering all the bases.

"Why a year?" Will asked quietly. He didn't want to consider other possibilities, like some twisted psycho was getting a sick satisfaction by butchering livestock while working up to something else, like a person.

"That's the question of the day," Zach responded.

Will wanted to conduct his own search of the property but Kelly needed him. It was frustrating that they had no idea who was doing this to the animals or why. Because that could mean the person or persons responsible could walk right past any one of them and no one would know different.

The small town of Jacobstown had always been a bedroom community. The biggest threat had always been poachers on the vast ranch lands. Whereas animals might have been at risk, people had always been considered safe. Most folks left their doors unlocked and until recently their keys in their vehicles.

"There any chance Kelly's situation could be related to the heifers?" Will didn't believe so, but it didn't hurt to get another opinion.

"I'm not seeing a connection," Zach stated.

"You said you just came from the main house?" That had been their parents' home and now served solely as the main offices for the Kent Ranch, KR.

"Mitch and Amber showed for the meeting. The others were already out patrolling the property, so I missed them, but they've been warned and will be fully briefed as soon as they make it back." Zach moved next to the granite island.

"Same leg," Will said.

"Yes."

"Fact one. The person, and I'm assuming this twisted bastard has to be a guy..." He looked to Zach for confirmation and got it in the form of a nod. Women serial killers almost always killed for resources and poison was most often their method of choice.

"This guy has a thing for the left hoof on a heifer and the month of December." With little else to go on, another twelve days could roll around without a clue. But they'd be ready next time. That was for damn sure. It was early December. Maybe that was significant. "Any idea how the suspect has been able to isolate a heifer from the herd? You already know we keep a tight head-count."

It was impossible to keep tabs on all of them when they were grazing.

Zach shook his head. "There were no footprints leading toward or away from the location. That makes twice."

"Where was she found?"

"About a mile from the last one up Rushing Creek," Zach answered.

"That's too close." This person also seemed to have a thing for water, or maybe it was just the creek. "We need to install cameras, build up security within a five-mile radius of those spots near Rushing Creek. The fact that there were no footprints both times makes me think this guy has planned these killings well in advance." Will looked to his cousin for confirmation of what he already knew. He'd been around law enforcement enough to be able to put the pieces together for himself.

"I agree." Zach set down his cup. "It takes planning to cover tracks this well."

"Hope something turns up on the library search. As much as I don't like the idea of a cult here in Jacobstown, the alternative is worse," Will admitted. He also took note of the fact that both cows had been heifers. No bulls. Did this person have a thing for torturing females?

Zach issued a sharp sigh. "We agree on that."

"Waiting a year requires patience," Will said. "Did the vet have an initial guess as to how long the heifer had been there?"

"A couple of days. Not more than a week," Zach said. "My deputies are overloaded at present but we'll dig deeper into this as soon as we free up resources. See if there are any stories from Jacobstown that crop up around this time frame that might be linked to this."

"Like what?" Will asked.

"Crimes that involve severing a leg or chopping off a foot." Zach blew out a breath. "Or accidents. Someone could've walked into an animal trap, lost a foot and been simmering with anger. That person might've decided to take his anger out on animals. Given both incidents happened here at KR leads me to believe they're connected to you and your family."

"There haven't been any accidents with anyone we know of," Will said. "Which doesn't rule out poachers. With the kind of acreage our family is responsible for we have no way of telling if something happened in a more remote area. I've heard of people chopping off a limb in order to survive a trap. Seems like we're throwing spaghetti against the wall to see if anything sticks."

"We have to consider every possibility no matter how remote the chances," Zach agreed. "Some of the biggest breakthroughs in cases come from thinking outside the box."

"You know we'll do our part to keep watch," Will stated. "Eyes and ears open and especially while we might still have an active shooter on the land."

"I don't have to remind you to keep your activities to research and not to get involved further than that, do I?" Zach said and Will caught the emphasis on the last few words as his cousin glanced at Kelly.

Will decided not to respond. Instead, he said, "This guy likes to have a water source nearby."

Zach paused for a second before continuing on. "Which is why I've put out word in the community to look for other animals near creeks and rivers. Anyone who finds a dead animal under any circumstances on their property should call me. I gave a description of what to look for but anything dealing with a paw or foot might help us out."

"That's as much as can be done right now without sending the town into a full panic." Will walked over to the laptop he kept on the counter.

"That'll most likely happen, anyway. Phone systems are jammed with callers, thanks to Mr. Hardaway." Zach's cell had buzzed almost nonstop in his pocket during the conversation.

"It'll make your jobs that much harder," Kelly said with an apologetic look toward Zach.

"I'd ask how you're doing but I don't want to insult you with the question after the day you had yesterday," Zach said to Kelly. "Hope you were able to get some rest."

Kelly smiled and Will noticed how much her face brightened even when the smile didn't reach her eyes. Her warmth reminded him so much of the reason he'd developed a crush on her all those years ago.

"I can honestly say that I've had better days," she said wryly. "Sheriff, I know that I'm not engaged to that man. I only have my word."

"Have any more of your memories come back?" She shot him a look of appreciation when he didn't contradict her.

She shook her head.

"I'm guessing there's no word on my cousin?" she asked.

It was Zach's turn to shake his head.

"Want to check your email? See what kind of communication you've had?" Part of Will didn't want to know, and especially if she remembered wrong and was in a relationship with Fletcher. Another stab of jealousy struck. One he had no right to own.

"That might help," she said as he turned the laptop toward her.

"I bet we could tell from my phone but since that's missing this will have to do." Kelly's fingers danced across the keyboard. She studied the screen. She turned to Zach. "I'll sign anything you want if it'll help speed along the process and enable you to gain access to my cell-phone records. Maybe my text messages could help us figure out what's going on."

"The offer is much appreciated. I know you're anxious to figure this out and so are we," Zach stated.

"Feels like my cousin's life might depend on getting the answers right," she said and Will could tell that she was being openly honest. The image of her in that wedding dress still burned holes in the backs of his eyes.

She pushed a ringlet of hair away from her face and scrolled through her emails.

"This one is interesting." She waved for Will to stand next to her. He moved closer, not really sure how he felt about potentially reading an intimate exchange between Fletcher and Kelly.

What he read was anything but. She was asking him to stop sending flowers and leave her alone.

"Look at the date." Kelly pointed.

"That was last year," he said.

"I remember dating him then," she said.

"How serious did it get between the two of you?" he asked. Again, he didn't want a front-row view to her relationship with Hardaway.

To be fair, he had a past. She had a past. And the

jealous reaction he was having was totally out of proportion to the situation they were in.

She clicked on the message, bringing the entire exchange into full view. "It says right here that I'm not interested in seeing him."

Sure enough, the words were right in front of his eyes. That didn't mean the two of them hadn't rekindled.

Kelly scrolled up. "See. That's the last email exchange we had."

Wasn't exactly proof but Will didn't want to erase the small satisfied smile toying with the corners of her pink lips. Hell, her lips weren't any of his business.

"Hold on. I didn't see this one before," Kelly said, pulling an email from her spam folder. "It's from Christina and it's marked yesterday morning."

That news got Zach's attention.

The three huddled around the laptop. This close, Kelly's clean and flowerlike scent filled his lungs.

The email read:

Remember when you first came to live with me what I said to you? K? It'll be okay. Be careful and watch your back. I'm serious. GAWIFN.

Love ya, girl!

"Any idea what this means?" Will asked, taking a step away from Kelly. Being this close was doing all kinds of inappropriate things to his senses—senses that he needed to keep clear if he intended to be any help with this investigation, which he did.

Kelly was shaking her head as she read it.

She scrolled down the list of emails, locating others Christina had sent. "She sent me this one a few days ago."

Hang in there, kiddo. It'll be over soon,

KTF,

C

"KTF means keep the faith. We used to say it to each other when life got rough." Moisture was gathering in her eyes.

"Why email? Wouldn't she just text you?" Will asked.

"Maybe she was afraid to," she responded.

"Can you go back to the other one for a second?" Will asked.

"What does that mean?" He motioned toward the string of capital letters.

Kelly just stared at the screen. "I wish I could tell you."

"There's another one." Will pointed. "How many email accounts did your cousin have?"

"She had one for work as a vet receptionist. And just one personal one that I knew about," she said, pulling up the note.

I know you saw us together the other day and again at the park. You shouldn't have said what you did.

Threatening to kill us both is childish. I hope you get it together and quit accusing me of trying to take Fletch away from you.

Christina

"That can't be from her," Kelly said, scrutinizing the screen. "First of all, that's not even how she talks. This is too—"

"Formal. Like someone was trying to make a grammar teacher happy," Will said in agreement.

"And you can look at every email she's ever sent me," she said to Zach. "She's never signed one of them with her whole name. She would never do that."

Zach nodded. "I have a tech guy who can analyze the messages. We can see where these emails originated from. It'll take time, but we can track the origins."

Will was grateful that Zach saw the email for what it was.

"Until we get this sorted out I'd advise you to lay low and stay somewhere I can contact you if needed," Zach said to Kelly.

"I want to be the first one notified when you find my cousin," Kelly stated. "But how? I don't have my cell phone anymore. I'm not going to my vintage jewelry shop anytime soon until my returning there is safe for everyone, especially my employees."

"I'll make sure she can be contacted," Will said to his cousin.

The comment elicited a disapproving look from Zach.

Chapter Nine

"There's a church about three miles from the scene of where Christina's car was abandoned. It advertises weddings on its website," Will said to Kelly. "That has to be the place where you were. It's out of Zach's jurisdiction. I'd like to speak to whoever was supposed to perform your ceremony. I have a few questions for the man."

"All I have to wear is your sister's clothes," Kelly stated.

"Do you want to go to your place and pick up more clothes?" he asked.

She raked her teeth over her bottom lip.

"I don't want to go back there until the gunman is caught," she admitted. "I'm sure Zach will give us an update if there's anything going on there that I should know about."

"We can bring extra security with us," he said.

"It's not worth putting people in danger for a couple of outfits. Do you think your sister would mind if I borrowed something else of hers?" she asked.

"Nah. I'll just see if she's around to lay something out for you. We can stop by the main house on our way out."

He picked up his cell and pulled up a contact. His place was a fifteen-minute drive from the main house.

Amber picked up on the second ring.

"Tell me you're okay," she said. For someone so young she sure did a lot of worrying.

"We are," he replied without going into much detail.

Amber sighed with relief. Her dramatic streak was their mother reborn. His baby sister had always reminded him of their mom. She was kind with animals and people, with a heart bigger than Texas. "Okay if Amber borrows clothes from you?

"She can have anything she needs."

"Thank you."

"I heard about what happened yesterday. That's scary, Will. Right here at KR, at our home." She paused for a few beats. "And now the heifer."

"We need extra security *now*."

"Mitch is calling in reinforcements," she informed him.

Between the heifer and the shooter, he wasn't taking security lightly. "Be on the lookout for anything suspicious and report anything you see. Okay?"

"You got it," Amber stated.

"Do your big brother a favor? Stay away from Rushing Creek until we sort this out?"

Amber agreed.

Because the nagging thought this sicko wasn't done yet stuck in Will's mind.

THE CHURCH CONSISTED OF a small chapel with an office to one side and a small room to the other. The smaller room was probably the bride's room that Kelly had mentioned to him.

"Good morning," a man said from behind. "Can I help you?"

Will and Kelly turned around and once the man, who was in his late forties or early fifties, got a good look at Kelly, his expression went from smiling to surprised.

"I'm Will Kent." Will offered a handshake.

"Roger Hanley. Pleasure to meet you." The pastor took Will's hand but never looked away from Kelly.

"You're already acquainted with my friend here," Will said, nodding toward Kelly.

The pastor nodded with a look of disapproval. "I'm afraid we've met."

Kelly stared blankly and Will tucked her behind him in order to bring the pastor's attention to him and stop the staring contest. He laced their fingers, a move the man seemed to notice.

"She was here yesterday," Will began.

"Yes, she was. In—" Pastor Hanley cocked his head to the side and lowered his gaze in a shame-on-you look "—pretty bad shape, in my estimation."

"It wasn't me," Kelly insisted.

Will squeezed her fingers in reassurance. It seemed to work when she relaxed her grip on his hand.

"We could use your help, sir," Will continued.

"What can I do for you?" the middle-aged pastor asked.

"We'd like to know who made the appointment yesterday," Will said.

"She doesn't know?" His hair was graying at the temples. He was short with a ruddy complexion. His round belly said he didn't miss a meal and his old, shiny suit said he didn't keep up with fashion.

"I'm afraid the wedding wasn't her idea. We're trying to trace this all back to figure out what happened," Will stated. He figured honesty was the best policy in this situation because they had no idea what she'd been doing there and why.

"She doesn't know?" he asked, his gray eyebrows knitting together in confusion.

"Could you walk us through the whole scenario?" he asked.

"I suppose." The pastor sighed as if he was releasing a heavy burden. "The phone call came in rather last-minute from Fletcher Hardaway. He explained that the pastor who was supposed to perform the service had to leave town suddenly and he was in need of a new location to marry his fiancée. I asked simply why the wedding had to go on. I wanted to know why it couldn't wait, but he offered a nice sum as a donation and said it would mean a lot to his fiancée if the ceremony could take place right away. He said it was even more important to have it here in Jacobstown since it's where she grew up. I tried to explain that technically this isn't Jacobstown, but he offered an even more generous sum for our inconvenience." He shrugged. "What was I supposed to do? Refuse such a generous offer? We can do a lot of good with the money that he offered here in our community. So, I agreed to perform the ceremony."

He glanced at Kelly with a disapproving look.

"I told him I couldn't perform the ceremony in good conscience once I saw the condition she was in," he continued. "Said I'd have to return the money or the two of you would have to come back another time."

Kelly shifted her weight to one side.

"What was his response to that?" Will asked. He realized that he'd been grinding his back teeth.

"He said that she had her heart set on this date and if I couldn't perform the ceremony that he'd go elsewhere," Pastor Hanley said. The man's shoulders slumped even more. Head down, glossy eyes, his posture was that of someone who felt defeated.

"Is that when you offered the bride's room?" she asked, shifting her weight to her other foot.

"Indeed." Again, he looked at her like she'd done something wrong. He seemed especially guarded with her around.

"Mind if the pastor and I talk outside?" Will asked Kelly.

She shook her head and her quick glance said that not only did she prefer it, but she was also uncomfortable being around this man.

Will already knew the pastor was making her nervous based on her warm palm. He'd maintained the connection to help her feel grounded. She still had patchy memories and they needed the pastor to fill in a few blanks.

"Mind if we step outside?" Will asked the pastor.

The man didn't stop long enough to agree. He started for the door.

Will followed and the pastor wheeled around as soon as the door closed behind them. The sky was gray. The air was muggy and storm clouds were rolling in.

"Everything okay, sir?" Will asked.

The pastor's ruddy complexion darkened.

"Fine. I just didn't appreciate seeing her again. The condition she was in yesterday was deplorable. To come into a house of worship in her state—"

"What was that exactly?" Will asked. His own curiosity piqued at the reaction the pastor had to seeing her again.

"Drunk," he said.

"She came here looking like she'd been drinking?" Will asked.

"We're not talking about a glass of chardonnay here," Pastor Hanley stated. He took a step and made a show of wobbling around. "I'm talking eyes glossy and barely able to stand up straight let alone take a sacred vow."

"I'm curious, sir. Did you get close enough to smell alcohol on her breath?" Will asked.

The pastor unfocused his gaze like he was looking inside for the answer. "No. I can't say that I was ever close enough to smell alcohol directly—"

"Who came with her?" Will asked.

"Her fiancé," the pastor replied.

"What did he look like?"

The pastor described Hardaway.

"Anyone else? A friend? Don't you have to have a witness in order to get married?" Will asked. Lacey had made all their wedding plans so he had no idea how this all worked. A little voice—the one that liked to remind him of all of his past mistakes—said that maybe she wouldn't have walked out if he'd been more involved in their life. It had been easier to stay overseas, fight the enemy he knew instead of the beast lurking within. Life in the military made sense. He wasn't William Kent's son. He was a soldier. He wasn't treated better or worse for his last name. It didn't come with expectations that he wasn't sure he could live up to.

By all accounts, there shouldn't be a devil to slay lurking inside Will. He'd grown up in a good family. He had the support of his parents, his siblings. Right?

But there'd always been something inside of him, a deep-seated desire to become his own man.

Stepping into a life that had already been laid out before him, all the hard work and accomplishments already done seemed… Hell, he didn't know the right word. Expected? Simple? Easy? Soft?

The ranch. The land. These things belonged to his father and mother. They'd done the difficult work, put in the sacrifice to make the ranch the success it was today.

Hell, Will even admired them for it. Even if their

legacy felt like a noose around his neck more often than not.

Granted, following in his father's bootsteps was never going to be easy. The man was a legend in this county. Everyone looked up to him, compared Will to him.

And the remarks had started early. In third grade he remembered his teacher telling him that Will was short for William, emphasis on the word *short*, after he'd spent too long taking a quiz.

At six feet three inches tall Will had never been short a day in his life. They both knew she was talking about expectations.

The only thing that had happened that was remotely up his alley at the ranch was the situation with the heifers. Now that they knew it hadn't been a one-off, he felt a renewed sense of purpose to solve the case before the mystery person struck again.

Being near a chapel must be the reason Will's mind was spinning. He refocused his attention on the pastor.

"Well, usually there are a few people at the very least. For this ceremony there would only be the two of them. My wife—" he motioned toward the farmhouse they'd passed at the front of the property "—was asked to step in for this wedding. She's at the store now."

Will didn't like hearing the word *wedding* in conjunction with Kelly and another man. It sat hot in his chest. He didn't have a claim on her. But that didn't stop his fool heart from betraying him at the mention.

"Was anyone else on the property other than you

and your wife?" Will started walking slowly, figuring there'd be some sign another vehicle was here.

"Not to my knowledge," the pastor stated.

There were multiple tire tracks leading to and from the chapel. Some of those tracks dug deep, which said someone had left in a hurry.

"Do you have a lot of business this time of year?" Will didn't make a spectacle out of noticing the fact that he also saw three sets of distinct men's shoe imprints.

"No. It's been slow recently. Our church is busier but we've had fewer bookings in the chapel this month. Not unusual for this time of year. Things pick up here around June."

Will figured the extra money being offered came in handy if wedding-chapel bookings were down.

"You said Mr. Hardaway called at the last minute," Will stated.

The pastor nodded. "That's right."

"It didn't seem suspicious to you that someone would call at the eleventh hour and then show up with a bride who could scarcely walk straight?"

One of the pastor's eyebrows shot up.

"I guess not. No. Not if I'm being honest. He had a good explanation," he said, but his hands were twisting together.

"And the two of them were alone?" he asked.

"Like I told you." The pastor's hands worked a little faster on his prayer beads.

"Did you know that a woman went missing yesterday?"

"No, I hadn't heard," he admitted.

"Really? That's odd. The sheriff said her car was abandoned on Farm Road 2623." Will pointed toward the gravel road. "Isn't that FM 2623 right there?"

"Yes, it is." The pastor's ruddy complexion turned a darker shade of red and purple. A few veins bulged in his neck.

"And you didn't hear anything?" Will asked.

"No. But thanks for telling me." The pastor's voice had an urgent, dismissive quality to it now. Like when someone was about to be ushered politely out the door for being too loud in church.

Did the man know more than he was saying? Will could tell a lot about a person by looking them square in the eye.

The pastor had a secret.

The tire tracks were a giveaway but the muscles in his left cheek twitched. He was uncomfortable with lying. But he was hiding something.

Again, Will thought about the exchange of money and how that muddied the waters. At least he'd fessed up to it. But then it would be easy enough to track through his bank account. There'd be no point in lying about a deposit of that size.

"How much money did Mr. Hardaway offer?" Will asked.

"Nine thousand, five hundred dollars," the pastor answered.

That was just south of the limit before the Feds forced the bank to report the deposit.

Just as the pastor touched Will's elbow, a move his mother had used in church to signal it was time to make an exit, a scream sounded from inside the chapel.

KELLY HAD BEEN sitting on a pew in the front of the chapel, where Will and the pastor had left her, when she felt a vise grip around her neck. She was forced to stand and move into the aisle. She tried to scream but a hand was covering her mouth.

Fire was everywhere around her. A familiar scent filled her lungs, causing her to choke as they burned. Gasoline.

As the wooden door to the chapel swung open bringing Will and the pastor into view, Tux lit a match and tossed it on top of the blaze.

Suddenly, fire was everywhere with smoke filling the small space. Kelly was dragged out the office door at the side of the building, helpless against the force threatening to crush her ribs.

It felt like an explosion had happened. What had caused it? Back draft?

More smoke burned Kelly's eyes and her nose as she was being forced away from the chapel and toward the woods.

"Get moving or Christina dies," the familiar male voice said. The scent of cheap pine-scented aftershave enveloped her.

The voice might be familiar but she had no idea who it belonged to. Tux wasn't someone she knew. She searched her memory bank for anyone she'd seen Christina with in recent months, but came up empty.

Kelly struggled to twist her head around and get

a look at his features. He was medium height compared to Will, she could tell that.

This guy had muscles. She tried squirming in order to catch a glimpse of his face.

Her eyes blurred and everything burned.

She wanted to scream for Will but the stranger's hand was over her mouth and he had known the one thing to say to keep her quiet.

He'd threatened Christina.

Hope that her cousin was still alive burst through Kelly's chest. If there was even a chance that Christina had survived, Kelly wouldn't risk making a sound.

Everything inside her wanted to shout to Will. Finding her childhood friend again had made pieces of her soul click together that she hadn't experienced since leaving Jacobstown.

She'd associated leaving town with losing her brother and father, and that was partly true. She would always miss them no matter how much of a screw-up her father was. She knew deep down that he never meant to hurt anyone with his schemes. Losing him and her baby brother had left a chasm, for sure, that no one else could fill.

But she'd felt that hole in her chest since before losing the two of them. Their deaths had only deepened the void.

"Where is she? Where's Christina?" Kelly choked out. Her voice wasn't more than a rasp, which would make screaming for help next to impossible, anyway.

"You're about to find out."

Kelly took a blow that knocked her to the ground. She brought down her hands to break her fall and heard a snap. Twig?

Pain shot up her arm.

That snapping sound was most likely her wrist.

Kelly rolled onto her back and kicked up at her attacker, crying out and holding onto her right wrist.

"You want to do this the hard way?" he growled, grabbing a handful of hair.

She managed to scream for Will as a fist flew toward her. She shifted to the left, taking a jab to her right cheekbone.

She shifted position again, trying to break out of his grasp.

"Help me," she shouted as a cloth was shoved toward her face.

The man dropped down on a bent right knee. He had a death grip on her hair—no doubt he'd take a fistful with him when this was over.

Wriggling left and then right, she tried desperately to break out of his grasp. The cloth covered her mouth before she managed to scoot away. There was a distinct scent. Something strong but that she had no reference base for.

The fist dragged her for a couple of feet before she realized where they were headed. He was forcing her toward a huge rock with jagged edges. It didn't take a rocket scientist to realize that man had the intention of slamming her into that rock in order to knock her out.

There was no way she could allow that to happen.

Kelly twisted around until her boots were pushing off the rock.

The man cursed.

He nailed her a couple more times and tried to slam her head against the hard earth. She struggled against his grip, using both hands to dig her fingernails into his meaty viselike grip.

He bit out a couple more harsh words between gritted teeth and nailed her with a knee straight into her ribs.

Air gushed out of her lungs and she struggled to catch her breath.

No matter how much she wiggled or moved, he countered. Her strength was wearing thin considering she was still recovering from the drugs. Exhaustion threatened but she knew from somewhere deep within that if she let this man win, she'd die.

If she could trade her life for her cousin's, there'd be no question about it. Christina had been Kelly's savior and there wasn't anything she wouldn't do or give for the woman who'd taken her in, given her a home and helped her figure out her life.

But that option was not on the table.

The very real possibility that Christina might already be dead struck. A fresh burst of adrenaline surged.

And Kelly dug deep to get off a kick to her attacker's face.

"Help me!" she screamed again. She shouted it

until her lungs ached and the man regained his position, his knee jammed into her back this time.

She could taste dirt as he shoved her neck into the ground.

Chapter Ten

Kelly had disappeared. Will was flat on his back, having pulled the pastor down to the ground in order to save him from the burst of flames from the back draft when they'd opened the wooden doors to the chapel.

"Are you okay?" Will shouted at the pastor, who was on the ground in a balled-up position crying and shaking.

The pastor glanced up at him and then frantically checked himself over, like he was checking to see if he'd been shot.

Will offered a hand-up.

The man was shaken but he looked fine physically.

"Earlier you said your wife is here," Will shouted over the roar of the fire.

"She's at the store," the pastor replied, still in obvious shock.

By contrast, blood thumped through Will's veins and the flood of adrenaline got him thinking clearly again.

"Where's your phone?" Will asked.

The pastor performed a quick search of his pockets and came up empty.

It was too late, anyway. Will already had his cell phone out and he was dialing 911. He requested a fire truck and the sheriff.

"Go in your house and lock the doors until help arrives," Will demanded, the soldier in him taking control of the situation.

The pastor started toward his place.

Will was wasting valuable time. He needed to find Kelly.

He darted around the burning building, using the full force of his adrenaline to pump his legs as fast as he could.

There was no sign of Kelly but he saw one of her boots on the ground. He ran to it and picked it up, tucking it under his arm.

The brush was thick and there were just enough trees to make seeing in a straight line impossible. There were more oaks than mesquites in this part of Texas.

Will dashed through them, using his hands to push off tree trunks and propel himself forward at a faster pace.

He pushed right and then left, darting through over and through the thick underbrush.

Where was she?

Smoke had gotten in his lungs and they burned. Normally, running at this pace would be no problem. Residual smoke was keeping him from busting full out. He wheezed.

And then he heard a scream. It was definitely a female's voice and he was headed in the opposite direction from where it was coming.

Will cursed and doubled back, bursting through the thicket and zeroing in on the area where the scream had come from.

There was more screaming and the sounds of a struggle.

He had no idea how many others were there but he recognized Kelly's voice immediately. His gaze continued to survey the area as he pushed his legs to run faster toward her.

More of his training kicked in as he drew near the sound. He slowed his pace, knowing full well that running straight to an injured party was a mistake that could cost both of them their lives.

Will pulled his knife from his ankle holder and gripped the steel handle. It had been custom-made to fit his hand. He crouched low and moved stealthily along the underbrush.

A man stood over Kelly. Good for her that she was fighting back. He was trying to force something over her mouth. A bandanna? Was it soaked with something like chloroform to knock her out? Make her pliable?

Someone wanted her alive and that worked in his favor.

The minute the guy got that bandanna over her mouth, secured, the fight drained from her.

A small flock of birds took flight to Will's left, higher in the canopy of leaves, but it caught her attacker's attention. His gaze surveyed the area below and it was only a matter of seconds before he'd locate Will.

So, Will charged toward him with his knife at the ready.

One look at Will and the guy dropped his hold on Kelly and took off running in the opposite direction. There was no way that Will could catch up to him and make sure Kelly was okay. The attacker was decently fast. If Will followed him, Kelly could end up alone and in more danger.

There was no doubt that Will could outrun the guy. He just couldn't leave Kelly in the middle of nowhere unconscious.

She was lying there, still, unmoving. And it was a knife to the center of Will's chest.

"Kelly," he said as he bolted toward her. He sheathed his knife, dropped to his knees beside her and checked for a pulse.

Got one.

A wave of relief washed over him as he realized her pulse was strong.

Every instinct he had screamed at him to get her out of there. Fast. That's exactly what he planned to do. He scooped her up and carried her until they were out of the woods.

By the time he reached the tree line leading to the chapel, emergency vehicles had swarmed the place.

There was an ambulance, thankfully.

Will charged toward the building, shouting for assistance.

He was so focused on getting help for Kelly that he forgot he was running into a crime scene.

A deputy moved behind a tree trunk and yelled, “Get your hands where I can see ’em.”

“She’s hurt. Unconscious.” Will maintained eye contact with the deputy. He didn’t want to make a quick movement or give the guy a reason to shoot. “I’m just going to set her down here on the grass. She needs medical attention. Please.”

“Go ahead,” the deputy instructed. His weapon was aimed at Will.

Gently, Will set Kelly on the yellow-green grass.

He immediately put his hands in the air, making sure he kept them where the deputy could see them at all times.

“I have a knife strapped to my ankle inside my jeans. Other than that, I’m not armed,” Will stated.

“Face on the ground and hands behind your back,” the deputy shouted. His high-pitched, agitated voice put Will on edge.

Will complied. “There’s a man getting away. He most likely started the fire in order to get to my friend and then took off when I gave chase.”

Will saw a pair of dull black shoes racing toward him and then the next thing he knew he had a sharp knee in his back, his hands were being jacked up behind him and zip cuffs were squeezing his wrists.

“What’s your name?” the agitated deputy shouted.

"Will Kent. I'm a witness," he stated as calmly as he could under the circumstances. "My cousin is the sheriff of Broward County. His name is Zach McWilliams."

He heard one of the deputies on his radio, calling to verify the information.

But the person he cared about most—Kelly—was being taken care of as he caught sight of a pair of EMTs running toward her.

"My apologies, sir," the deputy finally said as he and another one helped Will to his feet. They walked him toward a vehicle.

"He's getting away." Will nodded toward the tree line.

"Who is?" the deputy asked.

Will glanced at the man's shirt. A gold name tag read Daily. He was short, built and had brown hair and serious brown eyes.

"Deputy Daily, the person who started this fire and dragged my friend into the woods with the intention of kidnapping her is out there." Will made eyes toward the trees. "Her cousin is still missing and this is the second attempt to harm my friend in two days."

"Did this person have any weapons?" Deputy Daily asked.

"No gun. At least none that I could see." The conversation was moving in the right direction now.

"What did this person look like? Approximate height? Weight?" Daily asked.

Daily pulled out a small notepad and scribbled furiously as Will provided the information. The deputy spoke into his radio, alerting fellow officers of the potential danger and providing a description of the suspect.

"Why am I still cuffed?" Will asked as he leaned against the SUV. Kelly was being loaded into the back of an ambulance and he had every intention of following her to the hospital.

A man walked up wearing the same brown uniform as the other men with a patch on the arm that indicated he was the sheriff. His nametag read A. Vicar. He was stout with a clean-shaven face and a solid sheet of gray hair underneath his Stetson.

Deputy Daily introduced Will and the sheriff.

"This is a murder scene," Sheriff Vicar stated. "Nothing changes and no one leaves until I know exactly what happened."

"Hold on a second. Murder?" Will knew plain as day this was arson. The blaze roared behind him as volunteer fire crews worked to put out the flame. Unless… "Was there someone inside the church office?"

When he really thought about it, a secretary, janitor or gardener could've been trapped inside. The whole place swarmed with emergency personnel now and he realized they blocked his view of all the activity.

"No." The sheriff stared at him for a long moment, sizing up his reaction.

"Then, may I ask who?" Will thought about the pastor's wife. Had the same man who'd attacked Kelly gotten to Mrs. Hanley first? A thought struck. Had they found Christina?

"Pastor Hanley is the victim."

"Whoa. Hold on a minute, Sheriff. I was with the pastor not more than fifteen minutes ago and he was very much alive when I left him. Someone did this to him."

The sheriff took out a notepad as Will caught sight of a gurney with what looked like a zipped body bag on it being loaded into a second ambulance. Even though he'd seen death up close in the military, he'd never get comfortable with it. Loss of life, and especially in such an unnecessary manner, would always be a gut punch to Will. His thoughts immediately went to the pastor's wife, who would return from shopping to find that her life had changed in an instant.

The sheriff stared at Will, most likely gauging his reaction.

Vicar was of medium height and build with a little extra cushion around the middle. He wore all light brown, save for a dark belt with a silver buckle. Mirrored sunglasses shielded his eyes. "What makes you so sure he didn't perish in the fire or due to smoke inhalation?"

"Impossible. I left him standing right there." Will motioned toward the area in front of the chapel doors. Normally, he didn't give away what he was thinking but it was important for the sheriff to see his honest reactions.

The sheriff gave him a suspicious look. "With all due respect I don't comment about ongoing investigations with potential suspects."

"FAST FIVE" READER SURVEY

Your participation entitles you to:
✱ 4 Thank-You Gifts Worth Over $20!

Complete the survey in minutes.

Get 2 FREE Books

ur Thank-You Gifts include **2 FREE**
OOKS and **2 MYSTERY GIFTS**. There's
obligation to purchase anything!

See inside for details.

Please help make our

"Fast Five" Reader Survey

a success!

Dear Reader,

Since you are a lover of our books, your opinions are important to us... and so is your time.

That's why we made sure your **"FAST FIVE" READER SURVEY** can be completed in just a few minutes. Your answers to the five questions will help us remain at the forefront of women's fiction.

And, as a thank-you for participating, we'd like to send you **4 FREE THANK-YOU GIFTS!**

Enjoy your gifts with our appreciation,

Pam Powers

www.ReaderService.com

To get your
4 FREE THANK-YOU GIFTS:

✱ Quickly complete the "Fast Five" Reader Survey and return the insert.

▼ DETACH AND MAIL CARD TODAY! ▼

"FAST FIVE" READER SURVEY

1	Do you sometimes read a book a second or third time?	❍ Yes	❍ No
2	Do you often choose reading over other forms of entertainment such as television?	❍ Yes	❍ No
3	When you were a child, did someone regularly read aloud to you?	❍ Yes	❍ No
4	Do you sometimes take a book with you when you travel outside the home?	❍ Yes	❍ No
5	In addition to books, do you regularly read newspapers and magazines?	❍ Yes	❍ No

YES! I have completed the above Reader Survey. Please send me my 4 FREE GIFTS (gifts worth over $20 retail). I understand that I am under no obligation to buy anything, as explained on the back of this card.

❑ I prefer the regular-print edition 182/382 HDL GNTY

❑ I prefer the larger-print edition 199/399 HDL GNTY

FIRST NAME

LAST NAME

ADDRESS

APT.#

CITY

STATE/PROV.

ZIP/POSTAL CODE

Offer limited to one per household and not applicable to series that subscriber is currently receiving.
Your Privacy—The Reader Service is committed to protecting your privacy. Our Privacy Policy is available online at www.ReaderService.com or upon request from the Reader Service. We make a portion of our mailing list available to reputable third parties that offer products we believe may interest you. If you prefer that we not exchange your name with third parties, or if you wish to clarify or modify your communication preferences, please visit us at www.ReaderService.com/consumerschoice or write to us at Reader Service Preference Service, P.O. Box 9062, Buffalo, NY 14240-9062. Include your complete name and address.

HI-819-FF19

© 2019 HARLEQUIN ENTERPRISES LIMITED
® and ™ are trademarks owned and used by the trademark owner and/or its licensee. Printed in the U.S.A.

READER SERVICE—**Here's how it works:**

Accepting your 2 free Harlequin Intrigue® books and 2 free gifts (gifts valued at approximately $10.00 retail) places you under no obligation to buy anything. You may keep the books and gifts and return the shipping statement marked "cancel." If you do not cancel, about a month later we'll send you 6 additional books and bill you just $4.99 each for the regular-print edition or $5.99 each for the larger-print edition in the U.S. or $5.74 each for the regular-print edition or $6.49 each for the larger-print edition in Canada. That is a savings of at least 12% off the cover price. It's quite a bargain! Shipping and handling is just 50¢ per book in the U.S. and $1.25 per book in Canada*. You may cancel at any time, but if you choose to continue, every month we'll send you 6 more books, which you may either purchase at the discount price plus shipping and handling or return to us and cancel your subscription. *Terms and prices subject to change without notice. Prices do not include sales taxes which will be charged (if applicable) based on your state or country of residence. Canadian residents will be charged applicable taxes. Offer not valid in Quebec. Books received may not be as shown. All orders subject to approval. Credit or debit balances in a customer's account(s) may be offset by any other outstanding balance owed by or to the customer. Please allow 3 to 4 weeks for delivery. Offer available while quantities last.

◄ If offer card is missing write to: Reader Service, P.O. Box 1341, Buffalo, NY 14240-8531 or visit www.ReaderService.com ►

BUSINESS REPLY MAIL

FIRST-CLASS MAIL PERMIT NO. 717 BUFFALO, NY

POSTAGE WILL BE PAID BY ADDRESSEE

READER SERVICE
PO BOX 1341
BUFFALO NY 14240-8571

Will drew in a sharp breath. This situation had gone from bad to worse.

"Who are you to the injured party?" Vicar motioned toward the ambulance.

"Family friend," Will stated. "I brought her here."

"What was the reason for your visit?" Sheriff Vicar continued and Will didn't like this line of questioning or the focus to be on him and Kelly.

Will relayed what he'd said to Deputy Daily a few moments ago.

"You didn't answer my question." Vicar was wasting precious time and resources, focusing on the wrong people.

"My cousin will straighten out my involvement with this case," Will stated. "If you want me to answer any other questions, you'll have to go through my lawyer."

"I haven't Mirandized you," the sheriff stated.

"The problem is that you just stated that I was a suspect and not a witness. Until my classification changes and these cuffs come off, you can speak to me through my family's lawyer, Archie Davis the third." Will dropped the name on purpose—Davis was the most famous criminal defense lawyer in the state of Texas—and the sheriff's eyes flickered open a little wider.

"What did you say your name was again?" Dropping Davis's name got Vicar's full attention.

"My name is Will Kent."

The sheriff stopped writing. He tucked away his writing utensil as recognition dawned. "My apologies, Mr. Kent. If you'll turn around I'll get those cuffs off."

Will didn't normally drop his family name but in this case he needed to follow Kelly.

"You can interview me all you want at the hospital but I'm following that ambulance," Will stated. "She's in danger and needs protection from law enforcement. Can I count on you to provide round-the-clock security at the hospital or should I start making arrangements of my own?"

"That won't be necessary, Mr. Kent." Vicar's voice had an air of being offended. "My office is more than capable of protecting its witnesses."

The ambulance doors closed and the driver of the emergency vehicle shot a glance toward the sheriff.

Sheriff Vicar nodded. "My deputy will follow you to ensure safe passage through town, Mr. Kent."

"Thank you, sir." Will wasted no time jogging to his vehicle and hopping into the driver's seat.

The drive to the ER would take twenty-three minutes according to GPS. Using Bluetooth technology, Will phoned Zach in order to bring him up-to-date.

"It goes without saying that you had no business being there in the first place," Zach said to Will after hearing what had happened.

"I beg to differ," Will argued.

"You always were headstrong." Zach's sigh was heavy with worry.

"Maybe but someone followed us there or else the pastor tipped them off. I couldn't be sorrier that he's gone but there was something about him that didn't sit right from the get-go," Will stated.

"Like what?"

"He fessed up to taking a large donation to perform the ceremony. I think he may have tipped someone off to our arrival and potentially for more money," Will continued.

"What makes you think so?"

"He kept glancing at the door like he was expecting someone. He was nervous and he made a big deal out of Kelly being drunk or out of her mind or using drugs. I saw her not too long after he did and, yes, she did seem out of it, but she'd been drugged. She slurred some of her words and mostly came across as exhausted to me." Will remembered the scared look in her eyes, too. Why hadn't the pastor mentioned any of that when they'd spoken? "He swore that no one else was there but his wife, Kelly and Hardaway. So, where did Tux come from? He didn't just appear from nowhere. Kelly remembers him vividly and she absolutely knew he wasn't Fletcher. Based on her description he couldn't have been Hardaway or the pastor. And then not long after she left here a man chased her onto the ranch. Tux didn't fit the shooter's description. But you already know that part."

"Seems to me, then, we're looking for at least a couple of men," Zach said.

"The shooter either wasn't a good marksman or wasn't trying to kill Kelly," Will stated.

"Lucky for us you don't make a good target," Zach interjected.

Will thought about it. “I’m sure my experience helped but we were a huge target. She was in a white dress. It would be hard not to hit us if the man was trained.”

“Which most likely rules out a hired gun,” Zach stated. “I keep wanting to connect this back to Hardaway.”

“I don’t like him, either,” Will quickly added. A little too quickly. He hoped his cousin didn’t pick up on his protectiveness of Kelly. “Where is he?”

“I’ll find out if he has an alibi. Something tells me that he will.” Zach blew out a sharp breath.

“That’s what my gut says, too,” Will admitted.

“Did you get a look at the assailant?”

“He was too far away and took off in the opposite direction, so his back was to me.” Will wished there was more he could give aside from the general height and weight description he’d provided.

After a few minutes’ worth of lecture that Will had no business interviewing the pastor to begin with, a point Will conceded, Zach promised to intervene on Will’s behalf with Sheriff Vicar.

“He has a reputation for seeing the law as black and white,” Zach said. “He’s not the most cooperative with other departments, either.”

The brown brick hospital came into focus.

“I’m here.” Will pulled into the parking lot behind the ambulance, with the deputy who had been driving behind him also arriving.

“I’ll give Vicar a call. In the meantime, try to get a description of the assailant as soon as Kelly wakes. Getting her statement early on increases the chances she'll remember the little details that might just break this case apart."

"Will do, Zach." Will parked in the ER bay. "Thank you for everything you're doing."

"You know I'm always going to have your back," Zach said.

Will ended the call and jumped out of his vehicle.

This time, he followed the gurney inside the building. The EMTs moved quickly and that set off all his warning alarms.

He hoped like hell Kelly hadn't been given a stronger drug this time, something that would ensure she wouldn't wake up.

Chapter Eleven

Kelly opened her eyes and gave them a few seconds to adjust to the light streaming in from the window.

"You're awake." Will hopped to his feet and to the window, closing the blinds and plunging the room into a comfortable darkness.

"That's much better." Kelly heard how raspy her voice was. Her throat was so dry it might crack. She coughed. "How long have I been out?"

"A couple of hours." Will came to her side and sat on the edge of the bed. His gaze searched hers. She reached for him and he twined their fingers together.

"Do you need anything?" he asked. "Nurse? Water?"

His urgent tone warned her of the extent of her injuries.

She tried to sit up and winced in pain.

"No. Not yet. I'd rather know what happened first," she said, glancing at the wrap on her right wrist. "One minute I was waiting for you and the next I was being threatened and forced out of the chapel."

"First, Zach wanted me to ask if you can describe

the man who tried to abduct you." Will fished his cell from his pocket.

She rubbed her temples to stimulate her thoughts. "He was the guy from the other day in the tux. My back was turned to him but he smelled like cheap piney aftershave. It was strong, just like the other day. He was around the same height and build. As far as his face goes, I couldn't get a good look. He threatened to hurt Christina if I screamed."

Memories flooded back, not just from the chapel but all of them as Will texted the information to his cousin.

"They must've been watching us. How else did they know where we were? They want something from me. Otherwise they would just kill me."

"Why try to drug you?" Will asked.

"I mean, that's a really good question except maybe so they could take me somewhere else without a fight. All I can tell you is that Hardaway wanted to marry me last year, which surprised me because we hadn't been dating for long when he asked. We'd dated and I was fond of him at first," she said and could've sworn she felt Will's fingers twitch.

He looked at her and his eyes were unreadable. Did she want there to be something more than friendship between them? More than shared history? More than comfort in the moment?

Was she reaching for something or someone to hang onto while the only family she loved was missing? The familiarity that their relationship held had its appeal. She wanted a familiar shoulder to lean on right now. Kelly could handle things herself, but it was nice to have history with someone.

Or did the comfort come from that someone being Will Kent?

She'd never really let anyone in. Especially not as a child. There'd been a lot of fighting at home and Kelly felt like she was doing well to keep it together most of the time for her brother's sake. Their parents argued. Money had been tight. At times, the family barely got by.

The move to Fort Worth was supposed to bring them closer together. Her father had bragged about becoming part of something big, something that would change their financial circumstances for the better. Her mother could finally rent a chair for her cosmetology business.

Kelly remembered the late-night fights between her parents like they'd happened yesterday. She'd let her brother sleep in her room when he had nowhere else to turn. There was one that had been especially bad. The shouting pierced the walls. Sounds of objects breaking sent shivers down her spine to this day. She'd promised herself right then and there that she'd never struggle for a paycheck. Was that why she'd accepted Fletcher's advances early on? She'd known right away that he wasn't right for her. Fletcher was used to getting what he wanted. She'd seen that side of him from the beginning.

"My cousin seemed sure there was a link to the Hardaways and the accident that killed my father and brother."

"That's a shock. Why would she think that?" Eyes wide, Will tilted his head. "What do you think?"

"We did receive a big infusion of cash after we moved to Fort Worth. Now, I'm wondering if that cash came about because of a deal my father made with Mr. Hardaway. It's the only thing that makes sense." Christina seemed so sure that Kelly's father and the Hardaways had made a business connection. "Fletcher couldn't have been involved at the time. He would've been too young."

"I don't know how the Hardaways work as a family but we grew up involved in learning how to run the ranch."

"But your father was an honest man. He had nothing to hide," Kelly pointed out.

"How would your cousin have figured out the connection?"

"Christina had been searching online for sites that claimed 'found' money," she stated. "She couldn't find anything for herself so she started investigating the claim on my behalf and supposedly discovered that I owned land in Texas. It was probably not real but she started investigating and then mentioned Fletcher's family."

"Were the two of you dating at the time?" His gaze centered on the back of her hand.

"No. I'd already broken it off. I didn't see any point in moving forward with a relationship with him. I'm ashamed to admit it but I was there for the wrong reasons. Plus, I'd seen a darker side to him after he started letting his guard down around me. I realized there was more going on there than I could handle. After meeting his family I was even more put off," she admitted.

"So, why didn't it end there?" He used his thumb to draw circles on her palm. The move was most likely meant to be reassuring but everything about Will Kent was sex appeal and high adrenaline.

"It did. Until Christina came to me with an idea. She thought we could use his feelings for me to get close enough to him for her to get evidence on something she was cooking up. It was stupid but she said his family got involved with my father on a business deal. She didn't tell me all the details but asked me to get close to him again so she could access his files," Kelly said. "She said it would all make sense when she got what she was looking for."

"You didn't want to go along with it." Will studied her.

"Of course not. It sounds crazy to me even now," she said. "Crazy and embarrassing. I would never do anything like that for anyone but her. I figured that I owed her for taking me in when I was in high school. She saved my life and was all the family I had left."

"But she must've gotten something on the family and now they want to know if you know what it is," Will mused. His eyes had always been serious.

Everything that had happened up to now made sense when he said it like that.

"The problem is that Christina is missing," Kelly said. "She hasn't tried to make contact as far as I know but we don't have my cell records yet."

"Going to her apartment is out." He held up his phone. "We'll need to clue Zach in to what you remember about Tux and being drugged."

Kelly shook her head. "Christina was adamant about not bringing in law enforcement. She said Fletcher's family would figure her out and it would be over if anyone came around or started watching them, asking questions."

"It's a little late for that, don't you think?" Will asked but it was more statement than question.

He was one-hundred-percent right.

Tears threatened but she managed to hold them back.

Mostly, she realized that she wouldn't be alive right now if not for Will. He needed to know how much she appreciated his kindness.

"This is twice in two days that you've been there when I needed a friend." The last word came out a little stiffly. It was silly to think there could ever be more between them, even if an out-of-touch piece of her heart wanted more.

He lifted his chin, like he was doing what any decent man would.

Little did he know there'd been a shortage of decent men in Kelly's life.

She'd been told that she was beautiful and she'd been asked out plenty of times. But a *real* man, someone strong who could put others before his own needs—that was something in short supply.

The world needed more men like Will Kent.

"Thank you for making so many sacrifices in

order to help me." She held tight to his hand. "I don't know where I'd be right now if it wasn't for you but I'm fairly sure it wouldn't be anywhere I'd want to be. And I'm also pretty sure that I seem like a train wreck to you but I'm actually pretty normal."

More moisture gathered in her eyes. She wished she had a mirror or a hairbrush. Maybe a little makeup to put on to distract her. Those were out-of-place thoughts under the circumstances but she still wished she had those items. It was silly to think about her appearance right now. She told herself that she would look more credible if her hair wasn't wild but there was something more primal about her wishes.

Will thumbed away a rogue tear.

And then he leaned in and pressed a kiss to her lips. "I've never been especially fond of normal."

His hands came up to cradle her face. His touch was surprisingly gentle for a man with such rough hands—rough from a hard day's work on the ranch.

When he pulled back, his facade broke and for a split second she saw a deep storm of desire stirring in his eyes.

The kiss was most likely just a friendly gesture and she shouldn't put too much stock in it except that her lips ached to feel his against them again. Did he want her as much as she wanted him?

He dropped his hands and held onto her hand and there was so much comfort in his touch. The pad of his thumb worked her palm at a steady beat that was the most intimate and erotic experience she'd had in far too long.

"Tell me something normal about yourself," he said and she appreciated the redirection.

"I own a great place on 7th Street in Fort Worth. It's a small vintage jewelry store that specializes in turquoise pieces." Just talking about her little piece of the world made her smile. It felt good to smile for a change.

"Where do you get most of your stock?" he asked.

"I have a few artists in New Mexico for new pieces and then I buy from estates for others," she stated. She warmed at what looked a whole lot like pride in his smile. "Thanks for getting it, for getting me."

"You always did love finding things on the playground or at the park," he said. "You'd stick out your hand and your face shot rays of sunshine from your smile."

He seemed to catch himself when he glanced at the floor, then showed a more serious expression.

She liked the softer lines of his face when he relaxed. Will was an attractive man. He had the kind of straight, white teeth that would have women lining up to spend time with him. The fact that he was a Kent and probably one of the most eligible bachelors in Texas struck a jealous chord. Reality slapped her in the face.

Will Kent was out of her league.

"What about you? Where did you go to college?" She turned the tables.

"I didn't," he said on a chuckle when her eyes nearly shot out of her head. "My family understood when I told them I wanted to serve my country instead."

She let out a laugh that was more like a chortle.

"Maybe not right away," he added with another smirk that lifted the corner of his mouth on one side. "But they were always proud of me."

The way his mouth twisted had her brain muddled. Confusion drew her eyebrows together.

"Was it bad for your parents to be proud of you?"

He paused for a minute, intensifying his stare on her hand as he continued to draw circles on her palm.

"It's intense. Being a Kent," he admitted. He quickly added, "I'm grateful for my family, don't get me wrong. I loved my parents. We grew up with much more than most and I won't underplay it."

"But there were expectations, too," she added.

His eyes lit when he looked at her.

"Why do you say that?" His head cocked to one side.

"It just seems like our teachers were always reminding you of that. Anytime you made a mistake, and let's face it you made less than any other kid in the class, they'd mention your family," she stated.

"Yeah. But, hey, poor little rich kid, right?" He tried to joke his way out of the feelings that had to have been heavy on a boy.

"I wasn't thinking that," she said. "I never felt sorry for you."

She failed to mention what she *did* feel for him.

And her feelings now were most likely residual feelings from the crush she'd had on him in the past. They didn't know each other anymore. They weren't friends now and they'd gone in different directions.

"Thank you" was all he said.

WILL WAS GRATEFUL that Kelly didn't feel sorry for him. He especially didn't want that from her for reasons he didn't want to begin to break apart. Suffice it to say, he didn't feel sorry for himself, either.

Feeling sorry would be easier than the burden of feeling like he'd let down his parents. William Kent had left big boots to fill. As the second son, Will didn't walk to the same beat and that had always made him feel like a disappointment. Disappointing someone he couldn't care less about wasn't something that would keep him awake at night. Feeling like he'd let down the two people who cared most about him was a recipe for heartbreak.

Two years had passed since his father's death and it was too late to have the discussion that Will had been mulling over in his mind. He might not be cut out for the family ranch business. Mitch, his older brother, seemed natural with it all, as did Amber, his sister. What she'd done to bring the ranch to the leading edge of organic meat was nothing short of a miracle. She loved it and that made working long hours worth it to her.

Will missed the adrenaline rushes that came with battle. Being home made him feel strangely disconnected. He spent too much time in his head.

"Was it hard?" she asked and he tuned back into her.

"What?"

"Being in the military."

He issued a sharp breath. "Not for me."

The truth was that he didn't feel at home when he was home and he'd stopped feeling at home in the military, which was why he'd left. Lacey was supposed to be the answer but that hadn't exactly worked out as planned.

But those were not the issues he wanted to discuss. Like everything else, he shoved down the thoughts deep and forced a smile.

"But you don't like talking about it," she said.

"I don't see the point."

Will stood and walked over to the window.

"I thought I lost you back there, Kelly."

"I'm here now, Will."

"I didn't like it."

Chapter Twelve

"When was the last time you spoke to Zach?" Kelly asked Will, needing to focus on something else besides how much seeing him in pain crushed her heart. Besides, experience had taught her that she couldn't fix other people. She needed to bring her attention back to a problem she might be able to resolve, and didn't want to think about the consequences if she didn't.

Kelly would gladly trade places with Christina if it meant bringing her cousin back alive.

"On the way over." Will seemed to clue in when he said, "There's no news about Christina."

"There hasn't been any progress on the search?" she asked.

"Zach's doing his best. Resources are stretched thin. Volunteers are showing up to join the search. The fire most likely burned any evidence at the chapel."

She drew in a deep gulp of air.

"I hadn't thought about that but it makes sense. They get rid of evidence that way," she agreed.

Will leaned toward her. "There's something you should know."

She didn't like the sounds of that.

"The pastor was murdered."

It was as though the air had been sucked out of the room. "He's dead?"

Will nodded solemnly.

Even though he hadn't treated her very well she couldn't hate the man. She felt nothing but sorrow.

Trying to figure out what happened wouldn't bring back the pastor, but it could save other innocent lives.

"I remember that he mentioned taking extra money. Do you think he was covering for them?" she asked.

"More like for himself," Will stated. "Whoever is behind all this must've feared he would give them away."

"Don't churches get large cash donations all the time?" She had no idea how it worked. "I would think they made large cash deposits weekly after services, right?"

"Sounds reasonable. I haven't been in church since I was this tall." He put his hand about three feet off the floor. "But he admitted times have been tough so the deposit might not be consistent with the others lately. If someone in law enforcement is checking his books this could draw a red flag."

One look at him and she could tell there was more. "What else?"

"I'm a suspect."

"You?" She couldn't hide her shock. "No way. You saved me. That's all the EMTs could talk about. Sounds like you were pretty heroic," she said, feeling a red blush crawl up her neck.

"They would've done the same thing," he said, dismissing the notion of being a hero.

He was, though.

And he was probably getting sick and tired of putting his neck out for her considering they hadn't seen each other in more years than she cared to count.

"Listen, Will, you risked your life today and yesterday. This is serious and I know you have a life to get back to," she hedged. Nothing in her wanted to say those words but she felt she had to give him in an out.

"I was just about to ask if you wanted to come hang out at the ranch for a few days while you heal," he said. "That wrist took a bad hit and it might be hard to get around on your own."

"There's no way I can ask you to look after me, Will."

"Then don't ask. Take me up on my offer. It's simple."

Those words sounded like heaven except that her heart thumped louder when he was near and that made her nervous. She didn't want to care about another person as much as she could care about Will.

"Don't overthink it, Kelly." His deep timbre washed over her and through her.

There wasn't much she could refuse from Will

Kent. And that made being around him 24/7 sound like a huge risk.

It struck her that she was short on options unless she counted Fletcher Hardaway, but she suddenly had an idea.

"If I go to Fletcher's place, I might be able to figure out what happened to Christina," she reasoned.

"If he knows he's not going to tell you. But you might die and that's a risk I can't take," he said.

On second thought, he was right.

She wasn't stupid enough to try to strike out on her own.

"I appreciate the offer, Will," she said.

"Is that a yes?" he asked and there was a thread of underlying hope in his voice.

She nodded and he squeezed her hand.

"Is there any chance we could stop by Christina's place on the way?" she asked.

"Where's that?"

"In Bedford," she replied.

"We wouldn't be able to get past law enforcement if they're doing their jobs properly," he warned.

"I just want to see what the place looks like, you know," she said. "If someone's been there or searched through anything."

"The best I can do is call Zach and ask if he knows anything," he said.

"How does that work?" she asked. "I mean, that's not his jurisdiction, right?"

"There's a central database for counties to cooperate on crimes like these," he said. "Law enforcement will stay on the same page if everyone uses it. Plus, he has a network. He'll make some calls."

A crash in the hallway nearly stopped her heart.

Will popped to his feet and was at the door in a few seconds flat.

The man could move when he needed to. And he was smooth and stealthy, like a jaguar in motion.

"A cart spilled over." His voice was low. He stayed at the door. She could see his shadow on the floor from the dim light.

Adrenaline pumped through her and she could hear her heartbeat whoosh in her ears. Her fight-or-flight response jacked through the roof.

"It's time to go. I need to get out of here." Kelly threw off the blanket. It hurt to move. "I'm a sitting duck in here. Whoever is after me seems determined to get at me."

"Hold on." Will's voice washed over her, making her feel a calmness she shouldn't under the circumstances. "There's a security guard in the hallway."

At the very least, a rich and powerful man was after her.

Will helped her into her clothes and sneaked her out the door and down the stairs to his waiting vehicle while the guard chatted up the pretty nurses at the station.

So much for security.

"Have you thought about the fact that what was happening to me and Christina was being made to look like my fault and what happened at the chapel was made to look like yours?" she finally asked

Will as she settled into the front seat of his vehicle. He reached across her body to help her with the seat belt, since her wrist had a serious sprain but was fortunately not broken.

His hand brushed across her torso, sending more inappropriate sensual shivers racing across her skin. Will was like a campfire on a freezing night; there was so much warmth when she was around him and he was just as mesmerizing to look at.

"It crossed my mind." He finished buckling her in.

He took the driver's seat.

"If me and my cousin are gone, then it looks like I'm to blame because that's the underlying current here." She couldn't face the fact that Christina might already be dead. "And you're brought in to look like you're hurting people to protect me then whoever is behind this gets off scot-free."

"That's right," he admitted. "Except there's a wrinkle. We're alive and able to tell our sides of the story."

"Did you see the look on Fletcher's face when he realized who you were the other night?" she asked.

"He didn't seem thrilled," he said.

"Me and my cousin are nobodies. No one's going to notice if we're gone." It hurt to say those words but they were true.

"Nobody believes that," he argued. "And you're important to me."

"I just hate that I'm putting you in danger, Will." She let his statement run right past without allowing it to sink in. She couldn't afford to care even more about what he'd said.

"I hadn't thought about this before but taking you back to the ranch even with added security is putting my family at risk," he said.

He turned the key in the ignition.

"We can't go to my apartment," she said.

"Or any other obvious place," he stated as he put the vehicle in Reverse.

"What does that leave us to work with?" she asked.

"Not much."

WILL DROVE AROUND for an hour without a solid idea. He'd been toggling back and forth between using a cash-by-night motel option to keep them off the grid, although that would leave them vulnerable, to "borrowing" a fishing cabin from a buddy of his—a better option but not without risk.

"We need to stay close to Jacobstown," he said.

"Is there any way we can look for Christina?" There was so much fear in her voice. She seemed afraid to be disappointed.

"That might be too risky," he conceded. Alone, he could accomplish pretty much anything. Being out on the terrain he knew and loved—the land had never been the problem with living on the ranch—would be a no-brainer for him. But Kelly was injured and had no formal training.

His military experience could only go so far when it came to keeping her safe. The thought of leaving her with his family did cross his mind at one point, but the notion of bringing danger to the ranch was an unacceptable risk.

Right now, his training told him that being on the move was their best bet.

Kelly bit back a yawn. It was the third one in ten minutes.

"You can sleep," he said, reassuring her. "I'm not going anywhere. I'll be right here when you wake up."

"I can't. Besides, I'd rather keep you company." She leaned her head back and within five minutes had dozed off.

Will couldn't help but smile.

Kelly had always had a big heart and the best of intentions. She'd grown into a strong woman who ran a successful business.

Pride he had no right to own swelled in his chest.

Will could go days without sleep but it was smart to power-nap and keep up his strength. He didn't know for certain the enemy he faced. At first blush, it seemed like Fletcher. The Hardaways were a powerful Fort Worth family and Will couldn't ignore their influence. Mr. Hardaway could be involved. Fletcher could be a puppet.

If Christina had found information that could bring down the family, there was no length to which the Hardaways wouldn't go in order to keep it a secret.

But things done in darkness always came to light.

He pulled into the nearest rest stop and parked

near a light. The sun shield he put on the dashboard would block the light and unwanted people from looking in while he grabbed a few minutes of shut-eye.

He leaned back the seats as far as they could go, doing his best not to disturb Kelly. He'd had his vehicle custom-made so that the seats could lie flat. He never knew when he'd need a makeshift bed out on the ranch. Plenty of nights had been spent under the canopy of stars, sleeping in his vehicle. He'd also learned to keep a backpack full of supplies for those occasions, with essentials like coffee and toothpaste. He had power bars. The items would serve them well. Hell, when he really thought about it they could stay in his custom-made crossover vehicle for as long as they needed. He had a powerful satellite so he'd be able to pick up a signal from almost anywhere. There were showers and bathrooms on the highway.

His vehicle had cost a small fortune to customize. Will didn't throw his money around. But he'd spent more time in this than inside a house that felt empty with just him in it.

He pulled a blanket out of the back and placed a pillow gently underneath Kelly's head. He pushed a few buttons from the driver's seat and the back bench seat lowered to make a comfortable sleeping space.

She rolled over onto her side and tugged at his shirt.

At first, he thought she might be waking up, but her soft, even breathing said she was still asleep.

He rolled onto his side, leaving plenty of space in

between them—space that she quickly closed when she snuggled up against him.

He'd move if he wasn't afraid to wake her. She needed sleep.

Even if holding her felt a little too comfortable.

He needed to get a handle on his emotions.

But it was Kelly.

His heart clenched and he knew he was in trouble. The strong pull he felt toward her was most likely because of their shared history.

When was the last time he really connected with someone?

He knew the answer he *should* say. Lacey. His ex-fiancée should've stirred the emotions that Kelly did.

But his ex paled in comparison and that thought shocked the hell out of him.

He and Kelly had been kids when they'd connected all those years ago.

It was probably wishful thinking that any love could be that pure, that innocent.

Did he just use the word *love*?

Chapter Thirteen

Twenty minutes of shut-eye and Will was revived and ready to go. He gingerly slipped away from Kelly, careful not to hurt her bruised arms, and she stirred the second he could no longer feel the warmth of her body. She must've felt it, too.

He'd needed to put some space between them because when he woke with the smell of her hair—citrusy and clean—filling his senses, his body had reacted. Not exactly the wake-up call Kelly would be expecting, but with her soft curves pressed to his body the rest of him didn't seem to care about logic.

Since he'd never been a one-night stand kind of guy, letting his attraction to Kelly run away on its own wasn't his smartest move.

Sure, Will enjoyed sex for sex's sake as long as both parties agreed and there were no expectations of emotional attachments. But he preferred repeat performances when it was good, and multiple orgasms when it was great.

He had no doubt that sex with Kelly would blow his mind—

That's where Will stopped himself.

He didn't need to have that image before coffee. Or after. Or anytime.

Slipping outside with a few supplies, he moved to the picnic area in front of the vehicle. Lighting the small pilot stove, he heated water and made a cup of coffee. He sat on top of the picnic table and watched the sun rise. This was the only reason in his estimation to be up at the crack of dawn. He finished off a power bar and sipped the rest of his coffee. He pulled a bottle of water from his backpack and brushed his teeth. The rest stop had a proper restroom but he didn't want to take his eyes off his vehicle and leave Kelly vulnerable.

By the time he was on his second cup of coffee, the door opened.

He didn't want to notice how beautiful Kelly was in the morning or what a sight for sore eyes she was, like water to a thirsty soul.

Before he waxed too poetic, he said, "How about a cup of coffee?"

"Sounds like heaven." She stretched and yawned and he kept his focus away from the thin cotton material covering her breasts. "But I'd trade my car for a toothbrush and a shower right now."

He handed her a small bag of supplies. "Washroom's in there. It should be safe. You might come out smelling more like me than you want to." He motioned toward the bag. "But everything from soap to a razor's in there."

A small flicker of something passed behind her eyes. What? He had no idea.

And then he pulled out his Sig Sauer, which had been tucked in the back of his jeans. "And this is just in case the situation changes. Do you know how to handle a gun?"

"Dad made sure of it," she admitted.

Most folks who grew up in Texas knew their way around a weapon. And especially anyone who grew up in a town with ranchers. It was easier to shoot a menace than to try to trap one, since one of the heifers could end up snared instead.

Kelly took the offering and he ignored the frisson of heat that sent currents up his fingers with contact.

He wasn't exactly winning the war on being objective when it came to Kelly. And his body was almost a complete failure in keeping his attraction in check.

He'd deal with it.

She returned fifteen minutes later looking refreshed.

"It's amazing what a shower and clean teeth will do for the spirits," she declared, sitting next to him on the picnic table.

Shoulder-to-shoulder wasn't the best idea and he wondered if she felt the same effects from their contact.

He handed her a fresh cup of coffee and she mewled after her first sip.

"I was just thinking and I wanted to ask if we could swing by my apartment. Not to go inside, but is there any way we can see if anyone's been there?" she asked.

"It's possible but I'd work better on my own on surveillance and I don't want to leave you on your own. So, I haven't figured out how to accomplish that yet," he said.

"What about dropping me off at a crowded place? Like a restaurant or mall?" she offered.

"More women are taken in mall parking lots and grocery stores than almost any other places," he countered. How many times had Zach warned the girls in the family of those dangers? He was trying to make sure they kept up their guard. Of course, in a place like Jacobstown, there generally weren't many threats to speak of.

"I'd like to check on my store, too," she said before taking another sip of coffee. "This is amazing, by the way. Do I want to know how you're so good at making coffee on the run or why you keep toiletries on the ready?"

"Probably not." He laughed despite his somber mood. And that was the effect Kelly had on him. Sure, her presence comforted him in an odd way—odd because he'd never relied on anyone in the past, not even his family. Will had always been the lone wolf, preferring to take off for days on end and live on the land. Many of his favorite campsites were along Rushing Creek. And when Kelly was safe and her life returned to her, he needed to revisit those places to see if he could unearth any clues as to who was getting to the herd.

She glanced at him.

"I feel so lost without my cell phone," she admitted. "I mean really lost."

"You want mine?" He fished his out of his pocket and chucked it in the air.

She grabbed it in midair.

"Nice catch."

"What am I going to find on here? Sophie Lynn's number?" She bumped shoulders with him and laughed.

"I don't think I've spoken to her since sixth grade," he said.

"I'm pretty sure she'd still remember you with the way she used to follow us around but pretend not to," she teased.

With all the stress she'd been under it was good to see her laughing. In a corny way her laugh had a musical quality to it. Pride swelled in his chest that he'd been the one to put a smile on her face even if it was temporary.

"What should I check first?" She turned her attention to the screen and then pushed a button. "No password?"

"Why would I need one?"

"In case someone gets a hold of your phone." Her bewilderment amused him.

"It's always in my pocket," he stated, figuring that should clear this up.

She barked out a laugh.

"Who do you think will be able to take it from me?" he asked. "I'm a product of the US military and no one touches me that I don't allow. They'd have to pick it off my dead body."

He immediately regretted the choice of words given the situation.

"On second thought, you're probably right," she said after a small sigh. "I, on the other hand, need four levels of security on my phone."

"You've done okay so far," he said. "As far as keeping yourself safe. You've been through the ringer and you're still standing."

"That must be the pounding between my eyes," she said on a half laugh.

"Turns out..."

He reached into the backpack and produced a bottle of ibuprofen.

"No way. You seriously have everything, don't you?" She took a couple of pills and the bottle of water he had sitting next to them.

"You're amazing, Kelly," Will said. He hoped she realized how strong she was and especially after everything she'd been through.

"Thanks, Will." A red blush crawled up her cheeks as she set down the water bottle. "I'm amazed by you, too. It couldn't have been easy to chart your own course like you did and so young. You were always like that. Making your own decisions and then following through."

He pushed up from the picnic table and retrieved a power bar for her. "This will help you keep up your strength."

"Where are we going?" There was confusion in

her eyes at the change in subject and he didn't blame her one bit for it. The truth was that he didn't want to hear those words from her. Hearing them like that made him think he'd made the right choices and hadn't let down his family. Now they needed him more than ever and he wouldn't go rogue no matter how much he wanted to do his own thing. But for the past couple of days, a strange part of him felt more settled than he'd been in years. He told himself it was the familiar zing of adrenaline that came with putting himself in situations that put his life on the line. A part of him that he wanted to ignore said it had a helluva lot to do with seeing Kelly again.

He dismissed those unproductive thoughts. "I thought we might want to take a drive to downtown Fort Worth and check on your shop. We should be okay and I know you want to check on your shop. We'll just drive past it a couple of times and make sure nothing's gone awry."

"Sounds good." That wrinkle of confusion knitting her eyebrows together was a little too sexy than was good for his libido.

"And, Kelly?"

"Yes."

"Just so you know I won't be kissing you again."

KELLY DIDN'T WANT to think about kissing Will again, either. She'd fantasized about it far too much in the past twenty-four hours. She knew better than to want what wouldn't be good for her. She could argue the rich man/poor girl syndrome, but the truth was hidden much deeper than those surface concerns.

The bottom line was that she liked him more than was good for her. Will Kent would shatter her heart and she couldn't make herself vulnerable to anyone like that ever again. First of all, she didn't know how. Her losses were racking up and she'd built solid walls to protect herself from being hurt again.

When she really thought about it, safety was probably the reason she'd gone out with Fletcher in the first place. There'd never be a risk of falling in love with the guy, so he couldn't hurt her. The irony of that nearly cracked her in half. There was no risk of losing her heart to a man like Hardaway. Sure, he'd been charming in the beginning and there was a certain pull toward his underlying emotional unavailability that she couldn't deny. But dating him had been a mistake. One she wouldn't repeat if she had the chance.

There was so much she'd go back and change if she could.

In life there were no do-overs, so regret was a waste of energy.

Besides, she'd built a successful small business. She had a lot to be proud of in her life. So, why did it suddenly feel like she'd been living a half life?

An annoying voice in the back of her head said being with Will again made her notice what had been absent.

Kelly had never needed a man to complete her and she still didn't.

And yet being around Will made her aware that she'd been missing something in her life, or missing *out* on something.

She climbed into the crossover vehicle and secured herself in the passenger seat. Will helped with her seat belt.

It took almost an hour to drive to Fort Worth. They drove by her apartment building on North Main. Without going inside there wasn't much to see.

The store was next. It was still early and the store wouldn't open until ten o'clock.

Driving by, she could see that the windows were intact and there was very little foot traffic on Main, which was normal this early.

This area was her favorite part of Fort Worth.

Her shop was within walking distance of her apartment. They made a couple rounds searching for eyes suspicious people who might be watching her store.

"My employees will be worried when I don't check in with them, especially after Fletcher made such a public announcement about the attempted kidnapping," she said. "The reward he put out will bring out the crazies and muddy the waters of the actual investigation. Meanwhile, my cousin is out there, somewhere, either with the person trying to get to me or dead—"

"Or hiding out—safe but injured," he interjected.

She conceded his point.

"Or they could think you're lying low, which

would be the smart thing to do after a kidnapping or murder attempt," he stated.

"Getting shot at seems like a murder attempt to me," she said on a sharp sigh.

"Except that the shooter missed every time," he stated. "And the only reason he might've been shooting in the first place was to get me running and wear me out in order to get to you."

"I guess we have the United States government to thank for your physical fitness." That's as far as she wanted to think about his muscled body.

"I'd like to leave a note for my employees," she said.

He pulled over to the side of the road and grabbed a yellow legal pad from his console.

Kelly scribbled a note and started to make a grab for her seat belt.

"Not a good idea," he warned. "I'll do it."

She folded the note twice and then handed it to him. "There's a small space under the door that I've been meaning to weather-strip. Slide it in there and they should see it on the floor."

"It won't set off any motion detector alarms, will it?" he asked.

"Alarms are on the doors and windows. You'll be good."

He got out of the vehicle, tucked his chin to his chest and jogged past the storefront before circling back and stopping only long enough to slide the paper inside.

Kelly surveyed the street for any signs of movement as Will entered the vehicle.

"Considering that the motive for most murders is greed we need to find any information we can about your father's death," he said as he reclaimed the driver's seat. "See if we can figure out any possible links to the Hardaways or any of their holdings. I need to check in with my family so they know we're okay. They'll worry if they don't hear from me regularly. The shooter is the third time someone's been on the property illegally, not counting you," he said as they drove away.

"If Fletcher is involved he made a smart move in going public and offering a reward. It makes him seem sympathetic." She rolled the hem of her shirt in between her forefinger and thumb, a nervous tick, but it also gave her something to do besides sit and worry.

"He definitely created chaos. I'm guessing he hopes that'll take attention away from him and keep the sheriff's office busy." She thought the same thing.

"I have a bad feeling about all this." There. She'd said it. "I know I should stay positive—"

"Well, no one's asking you to be perfect," he interjected and there was so much compassion in his voice. "You care about your cousin, so it's only natural to have those thoughts every once in a while. The trick is not to get stuck there."

"Thank you. I know I said it before but I don't know what I'd do if you weren't here," she admitted.

He took his right hand off the wheel long enough to find her left and give a surprisingly gentle squeeze.

And then he pulled his hand away like he'd touched fire. His back stiffened and his muscles tensed.

"I keep thinking we're looking at this from the wrong angle. Life is about perspective and we're locked into one, checking on apartments and businesses. But then I got thinking the best way to solve any problem when I get stuck is to change up my perspective." He changed lanes. "Where would your cousin go if she left the scene on her own? Where's her safe spot?"

Chapter Fourteen

"Christina wouldn't come anywhere near here," Kelly said, motioning toward the downtown Fort Worth buildings. "She'd assume someone was watching these *if* she got away and could go somewhere."

"Based on the description of the vehicle and the amount of blood, we know she's injured." He didn't say the words *possibly gravely*, but they sat thick in the air.

Kelly tightened her grip on the hem of her shirt, working the fabric between her fingers and thumb.

And then it dawned on her.

"She used to take me under the bridge when I first came to live with her. We were in this small apartment with barely enough space for both of us and no air-conditioning. Imagine that in the Texas heat." She paused a beat. "So, we'd leave to get some air. There's this little white bridge leading to downtown from cow town. It's not far from here." Moisture gathered in her eyes at the memory. "We haven't been there in ages. She'd take me there when life got a little too real and we'd throw down a towel to sit on, eat French fries off some random dollar menu and dream about our futures. She might go there if she could get back to Fort Worth."

"It's worth a try." Will made a U-turn and headed back toward downtown from North Main.

The bridge wasn't more than five minutes away. A creek meandered around town. There was a jogging path with a greenbelt on one side. The path followed the creek, winding around and through the downtown area.

"I don't care what that last email suggested, I know in my heart that Christina and I were not at odds," she stated.

Will located a nearby parking lot and pulled into a spot. He cut the engine.

"I believe you," he said.

Those three words shouldn't be so important. They were. "Thank you, Will. That means a lot to me coming from you."

Kelly slipped out of the vehicle and stood in the sunlight. The sunshine warmed her face despite a chilly morning breeze. Temperatures in north Texas before Christmas could range from freezing rain to a warm sixty-degrees and the weather could change in a snap.

Life was no different.

She'd been doing fine before. Right?

And then life had turned on a dime.

Her business was having its best year since opening the doors five years ago. That first year had been a struggle to stay afloat. She'd worked ridiculous morning hours at a coffee house in order to make ends meet.

The second year was better, even though it wasn't good enough for her to quit her crazy-early gig. By the third year she could live off her business income and last year she'd hired two employees and an accountant. Life was looking up.

"What about the rest of your family?" Will asked, breaking into her reverie. "Would she contact any of them?"

"It's just us," Kelly said, hating how lonely that must sound to someone like Will, who had an abundance of siblings and extended family. "My mom ditched me when she remarried after my father and brother died. The last I heard she was living in California and was on her fourth husband. I'm not sure if I have any siblings. You already know what happened to the only brother I've ever known."

Will bowed his head and nodded.

"Christina and I are related on my dad's side. Once she took me in we just started figuring out everything together," she said. "From then on it was just the two of us against the world."

She smiled at the memory.

"We were rebels. Let me tell you. I was still in high school. I came to live with her after being passed around to relatives on my mom's side. Those were the dark years. Christina wasn't that much older than me. I came to live with her when I was fifteen and she was nineteen. She'd already been on her own for a year and I thought she knew just about everything. Looking back, we barely scraped by and she made sure I held up my end by going to school and working a part-time job to help buy food. My case worker helped us find resources to survive."

Will twined their fingers and they walked side by side to the walking trail.

"Between the two of us we were going to take on the world." Being here brought back so many fond memories with Christina.

"Sounds like you guys were well on your way," he said and there was more of that pride in his voice that she loved.

"We thought we were," she said. "But what did we know?"

"Christina never married?"

"She did. It only lasted a year. Turns out he was a bum. I don't think that's the word he used. I think he called himself a musician," she said on a laugh. "Don't get me wrong, I have nothing against actual musicians, people working to perfect their craft. And I don't have anything against someone being broke. I was in that position myself at one time."

"There's no shame in someone not having money," he added.

"Exactly. But they have to be working toward making it. You know?" She could feel that he did know even before he answered.

"Otherwise, they're just a freeloader," he agreed.

"My cousin worked two jobs to support them," she said on a frustrated sigh. "I think there was something especially kind about Christina. She would take someone in and help them get on their feet. She never gave up on people. He got involved in a bad scene after the divorce and went to prison. I think she'd been visiting him in Huntsville lately. She was secretive about it, though, so I can't be sure."

"Problem with some people is that they just want to be taken care of."

He found the path and they walked together, scanning the area for any signs Christina had been there.

"She finally figured out that he was freeloading when she came home early from her waitressing shift and found him in bed with a groupie," Kelly said. "I think that broke her. She swore off men for a long time after that. To make matters worse he tried to tell her that she owed him alimony. Thankfully, the state of Texas was having nothing to do with that."

As they approached the bridge, Kelly's heart squeezed. She took in a breath meant to fortify her and found no comfort in her surroundings.

Will's hand, though, kept her panic level down.

Relying on him was dangerous. Kelly had gotten where she was by relying on herself.

Why was it so hard to trust someone else?

She could blame it on bad experiences but, honestly, she'd never let anyone get close enough to really affect her if the relationship ended. A tub of ice cream. A box of Kleenex. A good rom-com movie. And she was over the worst of it.

Kelly pulled back her hand and stuffed it inside the pocket of her jeans as she walked.

If Will was put off by the move he didn't show it.

AFTER SCOURING THE ground for a solid hour and a half, Will's cell buzzed. He fished it out of his pocket and checked the screen.

"It's Zach."

He wasted no time on a perfunctory greeting. "What's going on, Zach?"

A deep sigh came across the line.

"Sheriff Vicar is about an hour away from issuing a warrant for your arrest," Zach said, his frustration evident in his sharp tone.

"Based on what evidence?" Will asked.

Kelly immediately shot a glance at him.

"I'm pretty sure all he has to go on is the fact that you were the last person at the scene who saw the pastor alive," he said.

"Aside from Kelly." This was ridiculous even for a by-the-book rigid sheriff like Vicar.

"He's not exactly listening to reason, and based on our family connection he all but accused me of covering your tracks." Zach issued another sharp sigh.

"A good lawyer would cut that story to pieces in minutes," Will insisted.

"I think he's of the opinion that we should arrest anyone who could possibly be involved and then let the courts sort out the details," Zach said.

"That's just bad law enforcement and a waste of taxpayer money." Again, Vicar didn't seem the type to worry about those details when he seemed to be on a rampage.

"I'm not defending him but let's face it. His

county doesn't see a lot of crime so he doesn't have the most experience dealing with these things," Zach admitted.

Jacobstown hadn't, either, but that didn't stop Zach from being a solid investigator.

"I didn't have much to offer by way of an argument," Zach said. "So, keep your nose clean and don't get picked up until I can find evidence to clear you."

This probably wasn't the time to notice a Fort Worth PD squad car coming off the bridge.

Will kept one eye on it in case he turned left and toward the parking lot.

"There's more," Zach stated and dread settled in Will's gut.

"Kelly's cell phone was recovered and Vicar's threatening to arrest her, too." Zach's frustration came through in his tone.

"He couldn't possibly have her password, and last time I checked a subpoena took a while to get from a judge," Will said.

"True. A subpoena for her cell records would take a long time. I have paperwork going through right now and don't expect it back for another few days," Zach stated. "But having a cell phone in hand and a murder investigation go a long way toward convincing a judge."

"But he doesn't even know what's on there. It could clear Kelly."

"Also true. But Vicar is an arrest-now-ask-questions-later sheriff," Zach warned.

"That's—"

Before Will could get too worked up, Zach interrupted.

"I just told you that to give you a heads-up. Those aren't even the biggest problem." Zach's ominous tone spread clouds over an otherwise sunny day.

And as much as Will didn't like the sound of anything he'd heard so far based on Zach's tone, things were about to get a helluva lot worse.

"Christina's body was found."

Chapter Fifteen

Kelly sank to her knees when Will delivered the news about Christina. The air thinned and her lungs clawed for oxygen. For the past forty-eight hours she'd been hanging on to a thin thread of hope that Christina was alive.

And what had Kelly been doing all this time?

Revisiting a childhood crush and getting lost in the feeling he provided that, somehow, despite all evidence to the contrary, suggested everything was going to turn out all right.

She and Christina would be reunited.

The mystery would be solved.

Bad people would go to jail.

That things hadn't turned out wasn't Will's fault. She knew that on some level. But being with him gave her dangerous hope that she couldn't afford.

"Vicar saw the report that Christina's blood was on the dress you wore," Will said.

"We were probably trying to get away together," Kelly argued.

"I know."

She wasn't stupid and had no intention of risking her life. If something happened to her, the jerk who did this to Christina would get away with it.

Kelly would never allow that to happen.

"Take me to Zach," she said to Will.

Will whispered so many words of comfort, of reassurance. And she could let herself get lost in those, in that fantasy that somehow seemed to work out for others.

Kelly's life didn't work that way, had never worked that way.

This temporary fantasy was about to end.

She sat quiet on the ride back to Jacobstown, grateful that Will hadn't tried to argue against returning. She was numb, so numb. Emotionally and physically drained.

Fletcher had won for the time being. He'd taken away the person who meant the most to her. A little voice in the back of her head wanted to argue that she'd let Will inside, too. She shut it down and shoved the thought deep inside.

As Will pulled into the parking lot of the sheriff's office, he said, "You should know that Vicar plans to arrest both of us."

"Good. Let him. He'll just be wasting valuable time and he won't get anywhere. Both you and I are innocent," she said with almost no emotion.

"I thought you should be prepared. Zach might not be able to shield us much longer," he said.

"There's no reason for you to walk through that door with me, Will."

He issued a grunt. “How do you calculate that?”

“I’m the reason you’re in this mess. You didn’t do anything wrong except try to help me. That’s your only crime. No good deed goes unpunished and all that.” Kelly bit back the tears trying to surface. She’d gotten this far in life alone and she would move forward the same way. Besides, it would only be a matter of time before Will cut his losses and walked away. He was a smart man, she figured, and when it came to gambling he’d see the losing hand that she was eventually.

He just needed a little nudge.

“Nostalgia has you going out on a limb to help an old friend, Will. I get that. But you can tick that box. You’ve been a freakin’ saint. Consider me helped and now it’s time for me to help myself. You said yourself if I don’t that makes me a freeloader,” she said with as much anger as she could muster. Mostly, she was angry at herself, at life, at her loss.

“If that’s how you see it, I can’t change your mind. I won’t try because it wouldn’t do any good.”

She opened the door, slipped out of his vehicle and walked away without looking back.

Part of her was grateful that he didn’t put up a fight because her heart wouldn’t be able to take it in her vulnerable state.

She walked inside the sheriff’s office as Will backed out of his parking spot.

Tears threatened to fall but she swallowed them.

An older woman jumped to her feet and made a beeline toward Kelly.

"I'm Ellen. Zach's secretary." Ellen wrapped her arms around Kelly in a warm greeting.

It almost melted some of the ice encasing Kelly's heart.

"Is the sheriff in?" Kelly asked, accepting the hug but still feeling nothing but a dull ache in her body. It was better than being numb.

"He's here." Ellen walked her down the hallway to the sheriff's office.

Kelly held out her hands, wrists up.

"Go ahead and arrest me."

Zach looked over at her from his screen. His shock outlined his features.

"I hope you know that I believe wholeheartedly in your innocence." There was so much honesty in his voice and frustration in his eyes. He looked over her shoulder and she immediately knew whom he was searching for.

"Will's not here." She left out the part where she'd forced him out of her life. "And he's not coming."

Zach's eyebrows knitted together in confusion but to his credit he didn't push her on the subject.

"He told you." Zach folded his hands and put them on his desk.

She nodded.

"I couldn't be sorrier for your loss, Kelly. I truly couldn't." He motioned toward the leather club chair opposite his massive oak desk.

His office was large and tastefully decorated with a masculine bent. The colors were deep browns accented by beige. There was a picture of the governor behind his desk flanked by an American flag and a Texas flag.

The desk was surprisingly clean and orderly. But then everything was stored on computers nowadays, it seemed, making stacks of papers a thing of the past.

Not surprising considering he most likely had witnesses, journalists and criminals coming through his office. He wouldn't want to leave other people's personal information where anyone could access it with a quick peek in a file.

Phones rang almost constantly in the next room and she realized that had everything to do with Fletcher.

Zach had always been one of the good guys and Will had spoken about his cousin many times with the utmost respect. And that's the reason she trusted him. If she was going to be arrested, she wanted him to be the one to do it.

"So are you going to arrest me or what?" Kelly asked.

"For someone who hasn't done anything wrong you sure seem to want to end up behind bars," Zach stated. His phone buzzed and he checked the screen.

She didn't realize she'd been holding her breath until he looked up and resumed talking.

"What's really going on with you, Kelly?"

THE CALL WILL had been expecting came an hour later than he'd wanted it to. He'd almost worn a hole in the living-room rug of his house. "Fill me in."

"I can't talk for long and, for the record, I don't like the feeling that I'm going behind someone's back." Zach's voice was a flood to dry plains.

"Point taken. But if she knows you're speaking to me she'll bolt or do something she might regret, like actually turn herself in to Vicar. We both know that could put her life at risk. We have no idea how deep these claws go into the criminal system." They'd already gone over it but Will would repeat himself a hundred times if it meant saving Kelly.

A deep sigh came over the line.

"That's why I called. I'm putting a protection detail on her. She's going on lockdown in her apartment, which I'm officially calling house arrest. He'll remand her into my custody and I gave my personal guarantee to appease Vicar."

"Those are a lot of hoops to jump through for someone who's innocent," Will said.

"There are never too many hoops to ensure justice is served and this was the best compromise. I agree county lockup isn't the right place for her. Someone could get to her before I have a chance to get her released," Zach said.

"There's no reason I can't be in Fort Worth as a second set of eyes," Will stated.

"I'd argue with you but instead I'll tell you to be careful and I'll let the officers on duty know her significant other will be on hand." Will appreciated his cousin for understanding his need to protect Kelly.

"We're good. Right?" Technically, Will was a fugitive but they both pretended not to notice it. In fact, Will had bought a throwaway cell so his number couldn't be traced, but he'd given the number to one person—Zach.

"Be careful out there," Zach warned.

"You, too, man," Will responded.

IT WAS DARK OUTSIDE. One of those pitch-black, cloudy nights that plunged the earth into shadows. Even in Texas, with its big open sky, the stars were impossible to see this evening.

Winds had kicked up in the last hour as Will patrolled Kelly's block on foot.

Access to her apartment came from the alley, a safety risk he would discuss with her once this whole ordeal was behind her.

Will wore his military green jacket in order to help him blend into the shadows. He had on a black ski hat pulled down to his eyebrows. His dark jeans blended in nicely with the dark night and his dark mood.

On this Wednesday night, the area was quiet, save for the occasional passerby.

An unmarked squad car sat at the mouth of the alley.

Will stood away from the streetlamp and popped a toothpick in his mouth.

Another unmarked car sat on the street, two storefronts down.

Headlights creeped into the alley, sending all of Will's warning flares shooting into the sky.

He glanced left and right.

The plainclothes officer at the end of the alley had his eyes set on the round headlights.

The vehicle stopped.

The engine idled.

Will couldn't get a look at the people inside since the headlights blurred his view.

Sticking to the shadows, Will crouched low and moved toward the vehicle to find a better vantage point.

Kelly's light had gone off hours ago and he imagined she was sleeping by now, unsuspecting. His fool heart tried to convince him that he missed her so much he ached, but he pushed aside that thought in favor of logic, which said they hadn't been around each other long enough for the pain he felt. Again, he tried to chalk up his reaction to missing something else in his life.

Blood pumped in his veins again and he felt alive. Will moved behind a row of trash cans, grateful the weather was cooler instead of being stuck in the blazing heat. The stench would've knocked him out and flies would've buzzed all around him in summer months.

Adrenaline had his instincts sharp.

He continued toward the end of the alley when the suspect put the vehicle in Reverse and started slowly backing away. Dammit. Will was too far away to get a look at who was inside. The alley was long and the vehicle spewed gravel. Will increased his pace but he was limited because he didn't want to risk moving too fast and giving away his position.

The unmarked car couldn't put on his lights or he'd risk scaring the driver and ruining the stakeout.

Will changed directions, jogging to the building behind him and along its side. He already knew there was an unmarked on the front of Kelly's street and he doubted the sedan driver would go there. The driver—Tux, or the shooter?—would most likely avoid that area now. He seemed to be exploring, feeling out the area.

With the news of Christina's body being found making headlines, the driver must have known the area would be hot.

Will watched as the driver disappeared down the road behind Kelly's apartment.

THE NEXT THREE DAYS and nights were quiet.

Not much happened and Will slept in fits and starts. One of his brothers would swing by to check on him or his sister would bring food.

On the fourth day, a small SUV with blacked-out windows made three laps, about one per hour. Someone looked to be casing the place.

Not seeing Kelly in days had Will in a foul mood.

Her cell records hadn't shed any light on what had happened.

There was so much on his mind, so much he wanted to say to her. It was a strange feeling to want to *talk* considering Will had never been one for lip service. But he missed the ease with which the two of them spoke.

There was no putting on airs with Kelly. She was down-to-earth and beautiful.

Of course, given what she was going through her intense side showed, but there'd been moments when she'd relaxed and laughed. Conversation was easy with her. Hell, having fun was easy with her. And part of him wished for lighter days so they could enjoy each other's company.

He almost laughed out loud at himself. Who was he kidding? He missed her and he didn't care how dark her mood was or what she was going through. There was something deep and primal in him that wanted to protect her, to be her calm in the storm.

Being together had distracted him. Based on the fact that she didn't want anything to do with him, he could only assume she didn't feel the same way. He would respect her wishes.

Call it Cowboy Code but he couldn't walk away until he knew she'd be all right.

Being separated from her, and her walking away, put a hole in his chest that he'd never felt before.

He realized that he should've felt this way when Lacey left him at the altar.

Granted, he hadn't especially liked the feeling. Rejection always stung. But much like an annoying bee sting, the swelling went down in a few days and he'd moved on.

The darnedest thing was happening to him now, though.

The mental image of Kelly in a wedding dress

with him standing next to her at the altar kept assaulting him.

The battle was on because he had no plans to get married at this point in his life.

His older brother, Mitch, had found happiness in marriage and he truly seemed the happiest that Will had ever seen him.

But marriage for Will couldn't be further from his mind.

So, why did the image of Kelly in that white dress wearing those boots keep replaying in his thoughts?

Chapter Sixteen

The blacked-out SUV crept along the back street for the fifth time in three hours. The tiny hairs on the back of Will's neck prickled. All his warning bells sounded and he could sense that something was going down this evening.

He left his post in the alley and tracked the SUV as it wound down a couple of streets.

The driver parked at Will Roger's Memorial Center in the far corner of the lot. A quick escape would be easy considering the driver could pop the curb and disappear into the complex of buildings and streets leaving the complex.

Three men exited the vehicle, all wearing dark clothing with different kinds of head covering that made getting a description difficult at night. One wore a hoodie, another wore a beanie and the third wore a ski mask.

It was chilly outside, to be sure, but not cold enough for the getups they had on.

Will kept to the bushes that lined the complex and snapped photos of the SUV, texting them to Zach.

His cousin had been working nonstop for a solid week, relying on catnaps to get him through the day.

When Will didn't get an immediate response, he assumed his cousin was asleep.

One of the men came around the back of the vehicle and used an automatic screwdriver to remove the license plate. He chucked it in the back of the SUV before clicking the doors locked.

Will snapped multiple pictures of what was going down and sent them to Zach. The photos were taking a long time to send, which wasn't uncommon when he overloaded the message system with multiple large files.

The images would go through at some point. Will caught a partial on the plate in Hoodie's hand before he'd tucked it in the back of the vehicle. That was a stroke of luck.

Hoodie, Beanie and Skier started walking right toward Will. He repositioned himself, ensuring they couldn't track his movement by crouching low and staying near the shrubs lining the parking lot. His thighs burned by the time the trio split up, each going in different directions.

Will texted the information to the officers he'd befriended—thanks to an introduction from his cousin—who were on tonight's watch.

Three men. Three directions. One Will. He didn't care for those numbers.

Nerve endings vibrating with tension, he decided to take bold measures. If the men were able to get to Kelly, he needed a way to track the vehicle. He assumed the plan was to kidnap her based on past attempts and figured that was the reason they'd switched to the larger vehicle with blacked-out windows.

The fact the men were still after Kelly wasn't good, especially after her cousin's body had surfaced. His heart fisted as he thought about the grim details of Christina's condition at the time of her death. The twisted SOB had tortured her until her body had given out. No matter how much violence Will had seen, he'd never get used to death.

The method these men had used to harm Christina could mean they'd gotten what they wanted from her and then discarded her. There were two outcomes with that scenario, neither of which he liked.

If the men no longer needed Christina, they'd want to make sure Kelly couldn't bring their dirty deeds to light. They had to assume she knew something or had something of theirs or they wouldn't still be after her. Another scenario he had to consider was that Christina had died before they got information out of her, in which case Kelly might be the only link to what they were looking for. Whatever the case, Will needed to be able to track this vehicle.

In the military, he'd have specialty equipment at his disposal. Out here, he'd have to wing it.

He stared at the cell phone in his hand. He needed to act fast because Hoodie, Beanie and Skier were getting farther from him and closer to Kelly. As much as he wanted law enforcement to handle this situation the proper way—the way that would land these criminals in jail where they belonged—Will wouldn't bet Kelly's life on their success and especially not after seeing what had happened to Christina.

Will activated the satellite map on his phone, allowing it to access his location. The cell battery was almost full, so he had that going for him. He put the sound on silent, no vibration. He couldn't risk the men walking up at the wrong time and hearing a call or text come in.

There were a lot of holes in this plan, not the least of which was the fact that he was about to be without his cell.

He became keenly aware of how much time he was losing but Kelly's life was on the line.

He fired off a text to let Zach and the other officers know what he was doing and where he was. At least the officers were warned about what was coming their way and they could send reinforcements to his location.

And then he crept toward the SUV, carefully checking behind every few steps of forward progress to ensure one of the men didn't round back to the vehicle. He knew that any pressure on the vehicle would engage its sensors. The last thing he needed was an air-splitting alarm blast to alert Hoodie, Beanie and Skier to the fact that someone was messing with their ride.

Will felt inside his pockets for something he could use to secure the cell to the vehicle, wishing he'd brought masking tape. Hell, while he was going all in why not wish for wire instead?

There wasn't anything useful in his pockets.

He glanced down at his tennis shoes and saw something he could use.

Will dropped down and untied his laces. He made a knot and secured them together to give him plenty of length to work with.

Stealthily, methodically, he continued making his way toward the SUV. Keeping low, he surveyed the area and then dropped onto his back and squirmed underneath the large vehicle. The wheel axle seemed a good place to tie the phone. It wouldn't overheat and burn through the lace.

Working quickly, Will tied off the phone and then wriggled out from underneath the vehicle. He'd lost valuable time but the move could save Kelly's life later.

Hopping to his feet, he stayed low as he cleared the bushes and moved toward Kelly's building. He thought about what she'd said about feeling lost without her phone. He could relate to the feeling. In an emergency, cell phones were a lifeline. Clearing her street, he doubled back and darted toward the alley.

There was no sign of Hoodie, Beanie or Skier.

The sobering reality was that Will wouldn't recognize them if they walked right past him without their head coverings.

It was almost seven o'clock in the morning. Rush hour would hit soon and it would be easier to get lost among foot traffic. The sun wouldn't rise for hours.

Will thought about his phone again. He had no way to get updates or communicate with the plainclothes officers on duty unless he walked over and tapped their windows. Definitely not a move he wanted to make under the circumstances.

A thought struck. Shift change would happen soon for Humphrey, the alley watch guard on tonight's shift. Even though the changes were down to a science, Will wondered if Hoodie, Beanie and Skier would try to take advantage in some way.

By now, this operation was a well-oiled machine but changes always exposed vulnerability.

And then, seemingly out of nowhere, an alarm sounded and the building lights started flashing.

Will cursed at the fire alarm.

The scent of smoke hit his nostrils, burning them, as he charged toward the building.

Confusion reigned the closer he got to the scene. People flooded the alley, coming from both the building and the houses behind in order to check out the emergency. He scanned the faces of every male for any signs of Hoodie, Beanie or Skier.

The truth was that they could be any one of these men. It would be impossible to distinguish who they were and Will faced the very real possibility that one of them could get away with Kelly.

Which also made him realize he was in the wrong spot. He spun around and started backtracking toward the SUV.

If he could put himself in the path of their getaway

vehicle he had a chance at intercepting them. That was his best play under the circumstances.

Will weaved through the thick crowd that had gathered and as soon as he was clear from all the people milling about, he broke into a dead run, keeping low and to the hedges as he rounded the corner.

Behind him, he heard a female voice cry for help. It wasn't Kelly but that didn't mean the person screaming couldn't be used to get to her.

Biting back a curse, Will doubled back.

At least the GPS could do its job and track the vehicle, if by chance one of the men got away with Kelly. Zach should be awake by now but it would take time for him to arrive. Even if Will was making a rookie mistake by running toward the sound of screaming he'd set a backup plan in motion to cover as many scenarios as possible.

And then there was another scream coming from a different direction. A second female voice wailed, her cries splitting the early morning air.

By the time the third cry came from yet another direction Will had figured out the plan. Divide and conquer.

But one of those female voices belonged to Kelly.

A crowd had gathered around a pair of people. Herd mentality had set in and not one person in the crowd was trying to save her.

Will pushed through the crowd and tackled the male—Skier—who was dragging a terrified-looking and -sounding woman in between two buildings.

And then Will saw why.

A shiny barrel.

One clean shot.

The crack of a bullet split the air as Will felt a flash of pain in his right shoulder.

Skier scooted away and used the frightened dark-haired woman to shield him as he ran.

Will pushed to his feet and charged after them until the sight of blood flowering on his white shirt stopped him in his tracks.

"Somebody do something," he groaned as he tried to keep forward momentum. He was losing a lot of blood and he knew that because he started feeling cold and his vision was blurring.

He could push through, dammit. He didn't want to give in but he could feel his body slowing. The more he pushed, the less progress he made.

Skier turned the corner and, in the blink of an eye, disappeared.

More shots were fired, this time from a different direction, from behind Will.

The red dot mushroomed and Will felt light-headed. He took a couple more steps as his legs weakened.

He felt his weight slam to the ground on the concrete surface before he blacked out.

A BULLET SPLIT the air so close to Kelly she winced. The officer who'd been escorting her muttered a curse word before getting on his radio.

The next words she heard were "Officer down. Backup requested."

Confirmation came through the squawking speaker hooked onto the shoulder strap of his shirt.

"You're hurt," Kelly said almost under her breath as the officer took a knee. "I'm so sorry."

"Stay down," he advised. "Help will be here shortly."

"I can't stick around," she said, knowing full well she'd be better off on her own now. A shooter had come close to hitting her and her flight instinct roared to life.

"Wait. Don't—"

She bolted into the crowd, figuring she needed to get lost in the sea of people at this point. Besides, if she drew attention away from the officer he had a chance at not being shot twice.

She knew that the shooter wanted her, not him.

Kelly had on her sleeping clothes, a T-shirt and leggings. She'd slipped on a pair of tennis shoes on her way out the door after the fire alarm had sounded. A bad feeling had enveloped her the second she heard the alarm bells roar.

The crowd should offer some insulation from whoever was looking at her, she thought, as she zipped in and out of the maze of people. Maybe she could slip into her shop. Forget that idea. She didn't have keys on her.

She could keep running until she figured it out, stay on the move. Wasn't that what Will had said was best in a situation like this?

Kelly sprinted out of the crowd. She glanced back to see if anyone was following before she cut around the corner. She collided with a male figure and literally bounced back two steps. The smell of cheap piney aftershave assaulted her, and a memory stirred.

The man wore dark clothes and a beanie. He pawed at her, catching her arms.

Then she looked into those dark eyes. More memories came crashing down around her and she recognized Tux's features.

His hands were like vise grips on her arms where his fingers dug into her skin. She twisted around and dropped down before popping up and rearing her fist back. She belted him square in the face but he just laughed. He turned his pug-nosed face to the side and spit blood with a smile. His amusement and stoic expression sent ripples of anger through her. Her cousin was dead, Kelly might be next and this guy thought it was all some kind of funny game.

At that, Kelly unleashed hell. She screamed and kicked even though she realized on some level that no one would hear her over the fire truck sirens.

Tux seemed to know it, too, based on the smirk he wore when he crushed her against his body and picked her up off her feet.

Kelly kicked and twisted her body but he only tightened his grip.

Instead of worrying for herself she thought about Will. She'd been thinking about him almost nonstop since the last time they'd spoken. Did she regret pushing him away? There was a simple answer to that question. Yes.

She hated the fact that if Tux got what he wanted

she would never see Will's face again. Never talk to him again. Never hear his voice.

Using her anger as fuel, she threw back her head and nailed Tux in the forehead.

That move got his attention.

His grip loosened enough for her to push away from him and bolt. Fear and adrenaline provided the boost she needed to outrun him.

Lungs and thighs burning, Kelly ran.

At one point, he was so close she could hear him behind her, panting.

Something inside her kicked in and she pushed her legs even harder, losing track of what street she was on or what was coming up next.

All she could do was run and run as fast as her legs would carry her. That was the only defense she had against Tux. There was too much chaos near her building to think anyone would notice her and she wasn't near it, anyway.

The man chasing her was strong and fast. He'd catch her if she didn't figure out another move. She thought about the police. If she saw an officer she'd run toward him.

For a split second, she thought about Will. As she wished he was there, she felt the familiar ache in her chest that she'd been experiencing for the past few days since walking away from him.

She realized now that cutting herself off from the only other person in the world that she cared about had been a mistake. She figured it didn't matter now.

Tux was gaining on her. She could hear his heavy panting from behind.

He wouldn't catch her if she could help it.

Could she round back to her apartment? Get close enough to scream for help and get attention before he caught her?

Kelly's lungs clawed for air and her thighs burned but she kept pushing. As long as she could keep some distance between her and Tux she had a chance at survival.

Her nose still hurt from the smell of his aftershave, so strong, so irritating.

And then she saw a building come into view.

Will Rogers Memorial Center. There was a parking garage behind the main building. She could seek refuge in there. She'd have to outsprint Tux and her energy was wearing thin but what other choice did she have? Her breath was coming out in gasps at this point and she wouldn't be able to keep up this pace much longer. She could only pray that Tux was weakening, too.

Kelly kept pushing. She could feel herself losing momentum. She pumped her arms in order to keep close to her original pace. Tux had to be tiring, as well, or he would've already caught her. Right? She could hear and feel him behind her but she couldn't risk turning around for a glance. One second could mean the difference between escape and capture.

Besides, she knew the complex they were coming up to and there'd be a good place to hide if she could get out of his sight for a few seconds. It would be so easy to get lost in there, she thought, as she sprinted across the parking lot.

Come on, she urged, hoping the internal pep talk would boost her spirits.

And then she felt the first swipe at her back. Tux grabbed her shirt but couldn't get a good enough grip to stop her. She broke away from his meaty hand but he was gaining on her.

She cut left, figuring she could sprint around the main building and then make her way through the maze toward the garage. It would be dark inside the parking structure and maybe she could get away.

It was the only idea that sparked.

Wouldn't there be security around a complex the size of this one?

Kelly could only pray she'd run into someone who could help as Tux made another attempt at the back of her shirt.

He got a better grip on it this time and so she shrugged out of her T-shirt. Now all she had on were leggings and a sports bra. She'd put the items on before bed every night just in case she had to wake and go. She also kept jogging shoes next to the door.

She thought about the fact that she hadn't had much more than a catnap since walking away from Will, too. Adrenaline would power her for the time being but that could only last so long.

Odd thoughts to have at the moment, given the circumstances. Her brain was going to the most random places. It was probably just protective instincts that had her circling back to thoughts of Will, and not the real soul-deep need she felt to see him again.

Kelly tried to shove those thoughts down deep, put them out of reach. They would do no good now. All she could think was how to get away from Tux.

The garage was in sight.

Her burning legs stumbled but she recovered and kept going.

And then she heard a grunt from behind.

Tux was closing in.

Chapter Seventeen

The multiple-story parking garage was so close. A distinct smell, like a cow pasture, filled her senses and she was so grateful it wasn't the stench of Tux's aftershave.

Kelly didn't know how much longer she could keep the pace. Her legs already threatened to give out again so she pumped her arms harder, searching for anything she could use as a weapon.

The sun was rising, bathing the parking lot in the first rays of morning light.

"You two. Stop," an authoritative voice ordered.

"Help me," she shouted between breaths but there was no way she was stopping. It was taking all the energy she had just to keep pushing her legs forward and she'd never find her stride again if she slowed now.

The sound of Tux's footsteps behind her stalled out.

And then she heard a shot.

Her heart squeezed and her legs weakened, but

she had to push ahead as she checked herself for signs of blood.

Fear slammed into her. This was not the time to fall apart. She could use this to her advantage because her fear brought another rush of adrenaline.

She could only hope the person—and she imagined he was security—would be all right. There'd been enough death around her.

Thoughts of Christina nearly crippled her.

Keep pushing.

Wasn't that what she'd always done when life got too real? That whole fake-it-'til-you-make-it saying had been her mantra. She'd gotten through a lot of rough patches repeating those words. Words were powerful.

Kelly couldn't risk looking back to see where Tux was but she couldn't hear his breathing behind her anymore. That frightened her. At least she'd known where he was when she could hear him. She half expected to hear another shot fired as she darted into the parking edifice and down a steep incline.

Her feet almost got in front of her. She had to slow her momentum enough to regain her balance or she'd skid face-first down the concrete slab.

Kelly wasn't sure how she managed; pure willpower was keeping her going at this point, but she finally hit even concrete flooring.

Lights turned on.

They must've been on an automatic system.

She darted toward the opposite end and almost

reached it when she heard huffing and puffing echo from the other side.

Tux was in the structure.

There was an escalator that was turned off. She sprinted toward it and took the metal steps two at a time.

At the top of the escalator was a lobby area attached to a conference center. All the lights seemed to be on the same automatic system, leaving an obvious trail for Tux to follow.

She bolted into the conference center. The room felt massive. Floor-to-ceiling curtains lined the wall next to her. For a split second she considered trying to hide. At least this room didn't have automatic lights.

It also meant she couldn't see very well.

She ran with her hand along the curtain, looking for an exit door.

Her heart squeezed when she heard the click of the doors opening where she'd just been. Tux was gaining on her.

There had to be an exit somewhere.

She hated to think what had happened to the security guard. Tears spilled out of her eyes for the man but she couldn't allow herself to give in to emotion. If she tumbled down that hill, she might as well stop running, turn around and let Tux take her away.

Panic set in.

And then she saw it.

A door.

A way out.

Kelly pushed a little harder to get to it before Tux could catch up. She could sense that he was getting closer and she could hear him breathing. And at this point, he was gasping like a fish on dry land.

She grabbed hold of the metal bar with both hands. It moved but the door didn't budge.

No. No. No.

Kelly threw her shoulder into the metal door.

Nothing.

She spun around in time to be whacked across the cheekbone by Tux's pistol.

The overwhelming piney cheap-smelling aftershave hit her at the same time his hands locked around her.

Adrenaline was fading and her body wouldn't give her anything to work with to fight back. She struggled but she realized that she wasn't putting up as much of a fight as she wanted to.

Still, if there was any way to wriggle out of his grip, she wouldn't hesitate. If she could get her mouth low enough to bite his arm, she would.

None of those opportunities came.

He kept one arm tight around her body, pinning her arms against her sides, and the other against the back of her head so she couldn't head-butt him again.

The stench of his aftershave made her cough. She dry-heaved, hoping she could at the very least vomit on him.

She tried to buck out of his grip several times but he tightened his arm until she thought her ribs would crack.

"I got her," he yelled next to her ear.

His meaty hands on her made her stomach turn.

She felt like a child being bounced up and down as Tux brought his prize to the others. And then she saw two more men standing next to an SUV.

The sun was cresting over the building, bathing the area in light.

Smoke billowed into the air from a couple of blocks away. Her apartment, her things, would be gone.

Another fire engine roared past, sights set on the blaze ahead.

"Watch out, she's a fighter," Tux warned.

One man grabbed her ankles as she tried to fire off a kick. The other jacked her hands behind her back. A few seconds later she heard the rip of duct tape. It was then being wound around her wrists. Pain shot from her right wrist up her arm to the point she felt light-headed. She wanted to scream out from the pain coming from her injury but she wouldn't give these men the satisfaction of knowing how badly they were hurting her.

Kelly bit back a string of swear words.

The next thing she knew duct tape was being wound around her mouth so she couldn't speak.

She was then lifted off her feet before being stuffed into the back of the SUV. Her hurt wrist screamed in pain.

A few tears leaked but she turned her face away from the men. She'd be damned before she'd let them see her cry. And even though she was scared half to death right now, she wouldn't show that, either.

These men had likely killed Christina.

If Kelly lived through this ordeal she'd see to it that each one of them spent the rest of his life behind bars. Justice for Christina was her new mantra.

She was so sorry that she hadn't been able to save her cousin.

Sadness threatened to overwhelm her but she couldn't allow that to happen. She couldn't afford to let her emotions run wild or confuse her thinking. She needed to plot an escape. She needed descriptions of the men in order to give to law enforcement later. And she needed to pop her head up and get her bearings no matter how much her body protested at the thought of moving.

Kelly knew this area of Fort Worth well. She'd been living and working here since leaving Jacobstown. One look and she could get an idea of where she was and maybe even where they were taking her. Although, the last part was a long shot.

The men in the front and middle seats spoke in low tones. She listened but couldn't make out their words over the low thump of rap music. Turning up the volume had most likely been on purpose on their part. They could speak without fear she'd hear.

Keeping her wits about her would keep her alive. That would be another new mantra. For her cousin's sake Kelly would remain calm. She couldn't bring Christina back but she could ensure these jerks never hurt another innocent person again.

Risking getting caught, she popped her head up. She had no idea the actual street they were on, but they'd diverted into a residential neighborhood and those she knew based on the style of houses. They hadn't gotten far from Will Rogers Memorial Center. The row of bungalow-style houses said they were to the east.

And then the volume of the music lowered as one of the men cursed.

"What's this?" the man she knew as Tux asked.

"How the hell do I know?" another man said. She recognized his voice. He'd been wearing a ski mask. It only made sense that one of the others was the shooter from Will's property. Based on size and build, it was most likely Skier.

Facing toward the back of the vehicle, she couldn't get a description. She lowered her head and maneuvered her body around—pain be damned—so she could get a better look. Pain from her right wrist shot up her arm with every move. She squeezed her eyes shut and thought about Christina, about what her cousin had endured.

"An officer's coming this way. You know what to do," Tux said.

Another one said, *"Now."*

The car tires spun in reverse. The driver had nailed the gas pedal. Kelly was tossed forward and slammed into the third-row bench seat.

Another curse. And then the SUV came to a hard stop.

Her body spiraled in the opposite direction and crashed hard into the metal gate.

She hit at an odd angle and more pain rocketed through her.

Everything hurt.

The back of her neck, her wrist, her arms.

"Cops back here, too," one of the men pointed out.

"Get the hell out of here," the other said.

The sound of doors opening and then shoes on pavement, running like mad, stunned her.

Police shouted loud commands but she couldn't grasp the words. Her brain split in a million pieces.

Had they just left her in the vehicle?

She half expected the SUV to explode with some bomb planted inside. Her imagination ran wild for a few seconds before she could rein it in and take control of the shock sucking her under.

She wriggled her jaw and pushed at the duct tape, using her tongue to loosen it. It took a few seconds for her plan to work.

"Help me," she shouted, afraid if she lifted her head, an officer might shoot her. "I'm here in the back and my hands are tied up. Somebody, please, help me."

"Let me see your hands," an officer shouted and she could tell that he wasn't getting close to the vehicle yet.

"I can't move them, sir. I've been abducted." She released a sob at hearing those words. "My name is Kelly Morgan." Another sob. "Please, don't shoot me."

Officers moved toward the vehicle. She could tell by the squawking radio noise growing closer.

It seemed to take forever for faces to appear and for the vehicle to be searched. Then an officer shouted, "Clear."

The back gate opened to three gun barrels pointed at her.

Once the officers got a good look, though, their attitudes changed.

"What did you say your name was, miss?" one of the officers asked.

Another was helping her out of the vehicle. Her legs gave as soon as her feet hit pavement but one of the officers grabbed her and helped her sit on the back of the SUV. Within a minute her wrists were free from duct tape, as were her legs and mouth.

Pain hit full force and she almost threw up.

"I'm Kelly Morgan. I was abducted."

An officer who identified himself as a supervisor approached. He said his name was Officer Riley.

"I've been briefed about your situation, Ms. Morgan," Officer Riley said. He held out a cell phone. "Sheriff McWilliams would like to speak to you."

Kelly took the offering using her newly freed left hand.

"I'm here. I'm fine," she stated after perfunctory greetings.

"I need to talk to you about Will." Kelly's stomach dropped at hearing those words. "He's been shot."

"What? How? He's not with me," she said, the shock of his statement not quite sinking in.

"He's been watching your place along with Fort

Worth PD," Zach informed her. "He was there tonight and chased one of the men, who then shot him."

This couldn't be happening. She kept waiting for the punch line, as though this was some cruel joke. It wasn't and she knew that on some level. Zach would never be that cruel. But her brain argued against the idea any of this could be true.

"He was taken to Fort Worth Memorial half an hour ago and is still in surgery," Zach continued. The more details he provided, the more real this felt even though her heart fought acceptance. "The surgeon said everything went better than expected."

"That's good news." Kelly was still trying to wrap her mind around everything. "Can I see him?"

"Officer Riley volunteered to escort you to the hospital. You can give your statement there," Zach told her. Those words were rain to parched lands.

"Thank you, Zach," she said. "You can't know how much I appreciate everything you've done for me."

"Your safety is thanks enough," he stated. "This part's none of my business but go easy on him."

Before they could end the call, an officer jogged up to Officer Riley.

"Sir." The word came out in a rasp. The officer's name badge read Riley. He leaned forward and put his hands on his knees, like he'd been running and was trying to get more air. "All three suspects have been apprehended."

A different officer, who had been searching the vehicle, pulled a shotgun from the back seat. He wore plastic gloves as he gathered evidence. "Sir, found something here."

Officer Riley excused himself as Kelly relayed the information to Zach that the men were in custody.

"What's going on now?" Zach asked.

"An officer found a shotgun in the SUV." Kelly shifted her weight from one foot to the other trying to keep upright. This was important but her mind was fixed on making sure Will was all right.

"I'll see if he can speed up the ballistics report and find out if it's the same shotgun that was used on the ranch," Zach said. "In the meantime, I know you want to see Will so I won't keep you."

She thanked him before ending the call.

Her heart hammered in her rib cage.

"Ma'am, medical personnel is on the way here. Are you sure you want to leave the scene before being cleared?" Officer Riley asked.

"I'll sign whatever kind of waiver you need me to, but I need to get to the hospital to see my friend *now*," she said.

"No need to sign anything. I'll take you right now." Officer Riley motioned for her to follow him to his cruiser.

She did and then climbed into the passenger seat.

A laptop attached to a metal platform had to be readjusted for her to be able to slide all the way in the seat.

Kelly was grateful when the officer turned on his lights and sirens.

The trip to the hospital went by in a flash, but felt like it took forever.

Kelly's aches and pains were starting to kick in. Adrenaline had faded but she refused to be tired. She'd racked up quite a few new bruises and scrapes. Her right wrist hurt like the dickens but she'd survived and the men who'd been chasing her were in custody.

None of them had been Fletcher Hardaway but that didn't mean his family wasn't involved in some way. They could be the conductors instead of musicians and the family could've been pulling the strings behind this whole operation.

Even knowing that the trio of frightening men was going to jail didn't relax Kelly's stressed nerves.

Officer Riley pulled up to the ER bay—an all-too-familiar place lately. He parked and told Kelly that he was happy to escort her.

She thanked him and took him up on his offer, figuring he'd be able to open doors faster than if she showed up alone.

Besides, she could use a hand walking.

Officer Riley offered his arm and she took it. He helped her into the ER. The check-in nurse stood as soon as she saw them.

"We're expected by a patient of yours," Officer Riley said.

She asked a few routine-sounding questions, punched a few keys into the computer and frowned. "I'm sorry to tell you that there was a complication during the surgery."

Chapter Eighteen

Kelly had given her statement to Officer Riley, whose shift had ended fifteen minutes ago. Officer Kirk had replaced the supervising officer. A nurse had checked her over and then a doctor. She'd collected a few more bandages after agreeing to an X-ray. She'd also visited the security guard who'd been grazed with a bullet at Will Rogers Memorial Center and had lost enough blood to pass out on the scene. Thankfully, he was going to make a full recovery.

Shock and adrenaline from the events had long ago faded, leaving her alone to deal with her pain. She didn't want to take a pill that might make her too tired to think straight and the pair of ibuprofen she'd swallowed couldn't make a dent in her discomfort. All of which paled in comparison to the pain of losing her cousin and the possibility of losing Will.

As she poured her third cup of coffee in the last half hour, a doctor walked through the double doors and into the waiting room.

Kelly's attention immediately shifted to the doctor, who walked straight toward her. He looked to be in his late thirties and had a runner's build. He had light brown hair and serious brown eyes. She and a member of Fort Worth PD were the only two in the room, so it wasn't difficult for him to know whom he was delivering news to.

The Kent family members were on the way.

"Mr. Kent is doing fine," the doctor immediately reassured her. "He's in recovery now and in stable condition."

The relief she felt was an understatement.

The doctor stood close to her and had a calm demeanor as he went on to explain that a bullet fragment had pinched off blood flow to his heart and had to be removed. "We were able to use noninvasive measures to retrieve it and are confident that we've now recovered every fragment."

He went on to explain how the tiniest piece of metal in the wrong place could disrupt Will's blood flow.

"When can I see him?" she asked, wringing her hands together for lack of anything better to do with them after setting down her coffee cup. At least drinking coffee had given her something to occupy her hands. Even with that and pacing the carpet, the last few hours had stretched on, feeling like the longest of her life.

"He's awake now and asking for you," the doctor said.

For her? Kelly didn't want to get inside her head at how much relief those words brought. After the way she'd treated him the last time, she worried that he'd never speak to her again. She thanked the doctor.

"Give us a little while until he's fully awake and a nurse will be by to take you to his room."

"Thank you," Kelly said.

After another series of laps around the room a nurse opened the door.

"He's ready to see you," she said to Kelly with a kind smile.

With every step toward his room, Kelly's heart felt like it swelled to the point that it might burst.

"He's right through those doors." The nurse pointed past the officer on duty, and the fact that Will needed someone to guard him was a physical punch. She'd brought this on him. She was the reason he'd been shot.

Kelly wasn't sure what she expected to see when she bolted into the room, but Will sitting up, legs thrown over the bed, with a smirk on his face wasn't it.

"Will." Seeing him like she was looking at him for the first time caused her breath to catch.

He was handsome in that rugged cowboy, drop-dead gorgeous way—although, he would laugh if he heard himself described as gorgeous.

"I thought they'd gotten to you." Worry lines creased his forehead as he motioned for her to come over to him.

"Are you supposed to be sitting up like this?" She moved next to him.

"No." He chuckled and then winced from movement. "Not especially."

"Maybe you should lie back down," she said as he took her hand in his and held it.

Hers was shaky but she was grateful that he didn't seem to notice or care. He had to have noticed, though, because not much got past Will Kent.

"Your family's on the way," she said.

"I told them to turn back. I'm getting out of here," he stated.

"You just got out of surgery, Will. Where else do you need to be?" she asked, not masking the shock in her voice. Sure, he was a tough cowboy type. But he needed to be reasonable.

"I'm making arrangements to recover at home," he said.

Oh. Right. A man with the Kent last name could afford the best in-home care.

The men after her had been caught. Maybe Will wanted to see her first so he could let her down easy, tell her goodbye.

"What did they do to you?" he asked through clenched teeth as he took inventory of her injuries.

She held up her right wrist.

"Stress fracture," she stated. "Basically, a lot of pain and not much can be done about it."

"I don't do worried," Will said to her. "And I was worried about you."

"The men who did this are in jail as we speak," Kelly said. Why did her chest deflate? Was it because now there was no reason for her and Will to be together.

"I'd like you to come back to the ranch and stay a few days, if you want to," he said, and it was the first time she'd heard uncertainty in Will Kent's voice.

"I would like that," she said and he gently squeezed her left hand. The move was reassuring.

"Let's get out of here." He tried to push to stand.

"I'm not sure that's a good idea." She tugged at his hand to get him to sit back down. "Let's head out after a little rest."

She motioned toward the pillows. "I'll lay down with you."

He smiled. "Bed's small but I think we can manage."

Kelly curled up against Will, wrapping her leg around his as he nestled her beside him.

Dangerous as the feeling might be, she felt a lot like she'd come home.

A COUPLE DAYS in the hospital and Will couldn't wait to get home. The minute he got clearance for release he insisted on being brought home immediately.

Waking in his own bed was a welcomed change. He glanced over at Kelly, who was sleeping next to him. Her warm body curled around his, molding perfectly to him.

For the first time in the new house, the place felt like home.

He also knew it was a mistake to let his emotions

get carried away with regard to her. But he could still handle it when she walked away from him. Right?

He'd made not needing someone else his life's work. Had he been shutting everyone out? Was that why he'd gone into the military instead of taking his place on the ranch? Maybe. Will had learned early on the less he needed people or their approval, the better.

It was a strange thought. One he couldn't exactly figure out why he'd had in the first place.

Deep down, he knew he wasn't perfect. That he'd let down his father and mother and his siblings, because as much as he loved the land he didn't enjoy the paperwork that came with running a ranch. Was he good with the animals? No question there. He was even better dealing with the cowboys on the range. Logging head made him want to poke out his eyes. He'd never been good at books or school. It wasn't that he was dumb. He had a decent IQ. His grades had been barely good enough to get into college and he could see the disappointment in his mother's eyes even if she tried to cover.

And he'd wanted to run as far away from the family business, from Jacobstown, as he could.

Was he searching for something?

An identity?

Something besides being a Kent?

Thinking about it now the answer was as plain as the nose on his face. He'd always been independent. He'd always felt the drive to go out and make his place in the world. The military had given him a place to grow and learn about himself. Since returning, he thought he was restless for the adrenaline, for the action.

But now he wasn't so sure that was the reason.

Lately, he thought a lot about Kelly.

Basically, he'd gone off the deep end and needed to find his way back.

Chapter Nineteen

"Good morning." Kelly stretched and yawned as she walked into the kitchen, where Will was putting on a pot of coffee.

He was recovering at lightning speed thanks to his fit body. He owed his fitness to the military for teaching him the discipline to wake early every morning and get in a workout before a long day's work on the ranch.

Kelly walked over to him and he wrapped his arms around her before kissing her forehead. He'd bought and had plenty of new clothing delivered since she'd lost much of hers in the fire. She would have to start thinking about rebuilding her life.

This close, her scent filled his senses and he muttered a curse for the effect she had on him. He was getting a little too used to waking up to her and it was weakness causing him to let it happen. When she walked away from him it was going to hurt like hell. She'd distanced herself once already and he'd been waiting for the other shoe to drop ever since.

"Dammit, Kelly." Will stared out the window. He

needed a distraction, something to take his mind off doing what would come so naturally to him with Kelly, what his body craved.

With her close he couldn't think straight. Especially with the way her sweet smell filled his lungs every time he took in a breath.

"What is it, Will? What's wrong?" He sensed the second she moved beside him.

She touched his shoulder and he instantly whirled around toward her. They stood inches apart but it felt like a cavern sat between them.

Hands at his side, he clenched and released his fists to keep from touching her.

"It's a bad idea to be here. Together. Alone."

"Why's that? It's me, Will. Your friend—"

He issued a grunt.

"What?"

"The thoughts I'm having about you right now don't count as friendly," he said.

She sucked in a breath, her breasts thrust forward and it was sexy as hell.

"I don't *want* to think about you when I shut my eyes at night. I don't want to *need* to know that you're all right, that nothing has happened to you. And I sure as hell don't want to hold you and take those pink lips of yours. But I'm about to no matter how much self-control I'm used to having in situations like these," he stated, watching her pulse thump at the base of her throat.

He wrapped his hand around her neck, resting the pad of his thumb where her pulse thumped out a rapid tattoo. Her full breasts lifted toward him with every sharp intake of air.

"You're beautiful," he grunted, knowing full well he should keep his thoughts to himself, but he lacked the ability with her so close.

Kelly took in a slow breath, one meant to fortify nerves, and he figured he was about to get the rejection he'd been expecting since bringing her here. The only reason she'd stayed this long was most likely to make sure he'd be okay. She'd mentioned more than once that she felt responsible for him being injured.

"Kiss me, Will."

He should've been taken aback by the request but it seemed like the most natural thing to do with the two of them standing there, bathing in the morning light coming through the slats of the miniblinds.

"That's probably not a good idea, Kelly."

She tugged at the tie holding her robe closed.

It opened enough to cause him to groan at the sight of her creamy complexion.

"I know that's not a good idea," he said, knowing that he should leave but his feet were rooted to the floor.

"Are you sure about that, Will?" Her violet eyes issued a dare.

The two of them stood there for a long moment, staring at each other.

And then Kelly finally said, "I don't care if any of this is a good idea or not. I've had a crush on you since grade school. I cried myself to sleep every night when we moved and not because we left Jacobstown or the only school I'd ever felt like I belonged. The only reason I ever felt like I belonged in the first place was because of you. I know you have feelings for me, Will. So, you can kiss me or I'll kiss you. I don't care. It's your choice."

She took a step toward him, shrugging out of her robe. It landed on the wood floor in a pile.

Will bit back a curse. She was intelligent, beautiful. He'd wanted to kiss her in fifth grade and had to admit that he thought about their first kiss the other day a little more than he wanted to admit to himself.

Her floral scent washed over him—it was a mix of soap and flowers and all that was springlike.

Will brought his hands up to rest on her shoulders. "This isn't easy for me. I know what I want but I also know what's right."

Will pressed his forehead to hers, taking in a deep breath. He closed his eyes. Kelly was intelligent and warm and beautiful. He'd be lying if he didn't want this to happen.

"I don't want to take advantage of the situation," he stated. "You're still tired. You've been to hell and back. You're vulnerable."

There were other reasons he couldn't bring himself to focus on, let alone speak out loud. She'd leave and, for the first time in his life, her walking out of his life might do him in.

Will didn't do fear.

She shot him a look that said she disagreed with pretty much everything he'd just said. Years ago, it had been like that between the two of them—one look and he could read her mind even though they'd been kids. The same had been true for her. They'd been able to tell what the other was thinking without drawn-out explanations. Sometimes it was written in her eyes. In this case it was the way her lips twisted—lips he didn't want to focus on too much at the moment or he might just claim them.

"I don't want to be treated like I might break, Will." Her hands were already touching him—his chest, his arms, roaming over his stomach. "I'm stronger than you're giving me credit for."

Damn. She was right. Kelly was one of the strongest people he knew. No matter what she'd been through, she pushed on. Situations that might crack a lesser person couldn't pull her under.

"I know my own mind. And, right now, it's begging for this to happen between us. If your body is strong enough."

"My body is just fine. If I sleep any more I won't for another month. You don't strike me as the one-night-stand type of person and I'm not sure that I have much else to give until I get my head on straight," he admitted. He'd never felt the need to talk a woman out of sex before. But this was Kelly and he knew the minute they crossed that boundary there'd be no going back. The thought he could lose her forever pierced a hole in his chest.

"What are you trying to protect me from exactly, Will? If you think I'm a virgin, you'd be wrong," she stated. "I'm a grown woman now. And this feels right to me."

And that was all the encouragement he needed. His body hummed with the need to be inside Kelly. But he'd force himself to wait, to take his sweet time and enjoy her beautiful body.

Kelly stepped toward Will and he grunted his approval. She had on nothing but pale pink silk panties.

"Pink was never my favorite color until right now," he practically growled.

Hearing Kelly's throaty laugh in response was even sexier.

He reached down to the hem of his shirt and she helped him pull it over his head. Her hands went to work, releasing him from his boxers.

He had to remind himself to slow down so he ran his finger along her jawline before dropping his hand and tracing her collarbone. He focused on each ridge and curve of her body as he memorized the feel of her silky skin.

"You have no idea how badly I've wanted to touch you since seeing you again," he said to her, and he could hear the huskiness in his own voice.

Her full breasts rose and fell as her breathing quickened, matching the drum of his own.

"I think I might," she countered, smoothing her hand along the ridges of his chest. "I've been thinking about that kiss the other day too much for my own good."

"And? What did you decide about it?" he asked.

She looked up at him with those intense and beautiful violet eyes.

"That I'd like to do it again. Here."

She pressed up to her tiptoes and brushed her lips against his.

"And here."

She feathered kisses in a trail down his chest. Her hands smoothed along his sensitized skin and he brought his hands up to take hers. He needed to stop her and make sure she understood they were entering a point of no return.

"Kelly."

Her gaze lifted to his where it locked on. Her violet eyes were glittery with need and he recognized that look. It was sexy as hell on the grown woman that Kelly had become.

It also told him that she wanted this to happen as much as he did.

Will issued a sharp sigh and then hauled her against his chest. His lips crushed down on hers in a kiss that had been missing that kind of passion for most of his life. He dipped his tongue in her mouth and swallowed her moan.

Her fingers gripped his shoulders as she pressed her body flush with his. Her full breasts against his solid walled chest. Her creamy skin that felt like silk against his body sent rockets of desire pulsing through him.

His body hummed with a need for release.

Her tongue delved inside his mouth. He captured her bottom lip between his teeth, sucking and biting with just enough pressure to heighten awareness.

Her pulse quickened, and he could feel it throb

against his thumbs as he held her arms at the wrists. Her tempo a perfect match.

Leading her to the bed, Will stopped at the nightstand to retrieve a condom. He ripped open the package with his teeth.

Kelly climbed onto the bed and helped position the condom on top of his stiff length. She hesitated at the tip of his shaft, tracing the tip with her finger before locking onto his gaze. She rolled the condom onto his erection.

Passion ignited like a forest fire, quickly spreading into a raging inferno as she pulled him on top of her.

He pressed up on his elbows and shifted his weight to one side.

"I want to look at you," he said. "You're beautiful."

The blush crawling up her neck at his compliment fueled the flame. She was beautiful but she didn't act the pretty-enough-to-be-a-beauty-queen part. Kelly had that rare combination of stunning natural beauty combined with a total lack of awareness about it. She was down-to-earth, giving and kind. But right now all he could focus on were those generous curves and that sexy-as-sin creamy skin.

He tucked a stray ringlet behind her ear, loving the way her wavy hair looked in the bright light coming in from the window.

He hooked a finger in her pink lacy numbers and made quick work of getting rid of those. And then he smoothed his hand across her stomach, stopping to cup her breast before rolling her nipple around his thumb and forefinger.

She gasped and moaned under his touch and he loved the way her body was reacting to him, nipples beading as she arched her back and her sweet round bottom pressed deeper into the mattress.

Her left hand came up to touch him but he caught her wrist.

"Do you trust me?" he asked.

She studied him as she told him she did. There was a hint of anticipation and excitement in her gaze and that got Will going even more. The need to be with her overrode rational thought.

He captured her mouth in a deep kiss.

And then he trailed his finger along the side of her rib cage to the curve of her hip.

Goose bumps rose on her skin and she slicked her tongue across her bottom lip, leaving a silky trail.

The urge to roll over and drive himself inside her was a physical ache.

But he didn't want this to end too soon.

Instead of acting on impulse, like a younger Will Kent would've, he slowed himself down and focused on the beauty of the long lines of her neck. He ran his finger down to the base, where her pulse thumped wildly.

His breathing quickened, too, matching her tempo as he kissed her. She parted her lips for him and he drove his tongue inside her mouth, tasting the sweetness as he trailed his finger down her stomach to her sweet heat.

"I want you, Will. Now." She tugged him until he repositioned on top of her. Her fingers dug into his back, clawing as she wrapped her legs around his midsection and he drove himself inside her.

"Will. More." He loved hearing the sound of his name roll off her tongue as he thrust himself deeper inside her sweet heat. She met him stroke for stroke as urgency built to the point that he was about to tip over the edge—an edge he wanted to jump off with her.

Her fingers dug deeper into his back and he pumped harder until he could feel her on the brink with him.

He dipped his tongue in her mouth.

She wriggled her hips, bucking him deeper inside until she exploded around him. When the last spasm was drained from her, he let himself go. Ecstasy enraptured him with every stroke as she teased him and bucked him deeper.

Heart pounding, breathing jagged, it was the most intense sexual experience in Will's life. It was so much more than a physical act. He was in deep, heart and soul, and there was nothing inside him that could regret it no matter how things turned out between them.

On his side, gasping for air, he felt better than he'd ever felt after a round of amazing sex. Check that, sex had never been *this* amazing before Kelly. And, granted, the area where he had surgery was going to kick his behind later. But it had definitely been worth it.

"There's blood on your bandage." Her eyes were huge.

He wasn't worried about physical scars.

"This changes things between us for me, Kelly."

WILL'S WORDS WERE so quiet Kelly wondered if she'd heard right.

She could recount her life in two parts—the time that existed before losing her father and brother, and the time that existed after. Until now, until Will.

Was she ready to start a new chapter that included Will?

Her heart said, "Yes."

Her mind wasn't as certain. It reminded her that death was always around her. She'd lost people she loved. She couldn't even think about Christina without tears springing to her eyes.

Could she include Will in her life now?

Kelly rolled onto her side and looked at Will. His even breathing and his chest moving up and down rhythmically said he was asleep.

His eyelids rolled back and forth.

Peaceful?

She knew he'd gone into the military. There was so much regret in his eyes when he talked about his family.

She had demons.

He had demons.

For a split second she thought about fifth grade. Their fingers linked together on the playground as they ran around, living in their own world.

The sense that everything in the world would somehow be okay, that everything would magically work out, came with that link then as much as now.

Would it, though?

Chapter Twenty

Will's cell buzzed, waking him from a deep sleep. He forced himself to sit up and snatched his cell from his nightstand. He checked the screen and then answered the call. "What's up, Zach?"

"The ballistics report came in. The shell casings found on the ranch match the shotgun from the SUV," his cousin said. "We have the right guys in custody. We were also able to trace the last two emails sent from Christina to Kelly to one of the perps' laptops."

There was something in his voice—hesitation?

"That's good news, right?" Will asked after relaying the information to Kelly, who'd pushed up to sitting. He put the phone on speaker so she could directly hear, not caring if Zach wondered what Kelly was doing by his side this morning.

"It should be," Zach said.

"But you don't think it is?" Kelly asked.

"I'm not yet ready to close the books even if other investigators are," Zach said.

"What did they give as a reason?" Will asked,

thinking back to the number of conversations he'd had with Zach about motive. Crime always came down to motive.

"The guys said they'd become fixated on the women, who they'd seen out together on several occasions," he said. "We searched each of their residences and confiscated several technology devices where we found multiple pictures in a central cloud storage that had been uploaded from phones belonging to each of them."

"Sounds damning," Will said.

"The men had obviously been watching Ms. Foxwood and Kelly for some time." Zach issued a pregnant pause. "This is just me speaking, of course, but I'm not one-hundred-percent certain this was an obsession. Those pictures tend to be of a victim at home wearing less."

It dawned on Will. "Sounds like these photos were surveillance-related."

"In my opinion," Zach said. "The other investigators don't agree. To them, this case is closed."

"I'm guessing that means there aren't any connections to Hardaway," Will said.

"None that we could find." Zach paused again. "From an official standpoint this case is closed but personally I have no plans to abandon the investigation. The first place I intend to look is the Hardaway family."

"Mr. Hardaway will have lawyers in order to make sure his family name is protected," Kelly said.

"He's not stupid and he'll make it as difficult as possible to pin him to any criminal activity."

"I wish we knew what your cousin found on him," Zach said.

"I do, too," Kelly agreed.

"Even with these guys locked up and eyes on the family I'd play it safe over the next few days until the dust settles," Zach advised.

"We'll be taking it easy," Will agreed, especially considering they both needed time to heal from their injuries, physical and emotional.

"I'll keep you posted," Zach said. "Before I go, I thought you should know we got a hit on our bulletin about the heifers and the call for other animal sightings. A report came in that a rabbit was found missing a left paw. It had been severed and left to bleed out with no obvious signs of being caught in a trap."

"Where?" Will asked.

"On the Jasper ranch," Zach supplied.

"Where Christina's car was found," Will said.

"That's right. The rabbit was found when volunteers were scouring the area looking for her," Zach stated.

"When was the rabbit killed?" Will asked.

"We have a forensic expert looking at it right now," Zach said. "Suffice it to say it had been there for some time before it was found."

Will didn't need to speak his thoughts out loud. He and Zach both knew this could influence the killer's timeline, and, therefore, upset the theory he only struck in December. "Any initial guesses? Months? Years?"

"The primary finding points to months. At this point, we're not expecting a definitive answer, just a ballpark," Zach said.

"So much death around," Kelly muttered so low Will almost didn't hear her. "I should never have agreed to go along with Christina's plan. It was stupid of me to think we could fool one of the wealthiest families in Texas. She would be alive right now—"

Her breath hitched and she couldn't seem to finish her sentence.

"None of what has happened is your fault, Kelly," Zach said before Will could. "If you hadn't gone along with her she would've gone about it another way. The end result would still be the same but we'd be no closer to figuring out who killed her and why."

"I should've asked more questions. I should've insisted she tell me what she thought she had on him," she continued.

"From what I've heard about your cousin so far she wouldn't have told you. She was trying to protect you," Zach said. "I know I've said it before but I'm sorry for your loss. Christina sounded like a brave and wonderful person."

Will thumbed away a tear rolling down Kelly's cheek.

"It's so hard to believe that she's gone and I'm here," Kelly said.

On so many levels, Will could relate to the pain

of loss she felt. Had he come to terms with losing his parents? Would he ever be able to?

Losing Lacey had chipped away the last of his ability to put himself out there with anyone.

Until Kelly.

But what did that mean exactly?

So much senseless loss, Kelly thought as Will ended the call with his cousin. Pain tore through her again at thinking about how much Christina had suffered.

Kelly couldn't imagine surviving any of this without Will, but she knew that she would if she had to. Pushing through pain and putting one-hundred-percent focus on her goals had gotten her through very dark days and would again. She knew the day would soon come when life would go back to normal. She almost laughed out loud at the irony in that thought because life would never be the same without Christina.

Still, a time would come when Kelly would go back to her world and Will would go back to his.

"I remember you told me in fifth grade that you wanted to leave Jacobstown. You had all these plans never to come back." She wondered if he regretted being here and especially after all that had happened in recent weeks.

"Let's see. What was I going to be back then? A fire jumper in Colorado?" he said and she appreciated lighter conversation after feeling a boulder had lodged itself in between her ribs and sat heavy on her chest.

"That's right. Most boys at that age wanted to be a fireman. A job that's dangerous enough. But you wanted to push the limits and jump into a fire from above," she said. "Drop into a cloud of smoke and live to tell about it."

"What can I say?" he asked. "I was always the adventurous type."

"Can't say that I'm surprised you signed up for the military instead," she said.

"It seemed a good way to give back to the country that's been so good to me and my family." She felt his chest puff with pride.

"How's it been since you left a job you loved?" she asked.

"In a word? Boring." He chuckled, a low rumble in his chest. "I love the land and I love the animals. Being here with family is good for me. But the paperwork involved in running a ranch is a nightmare. I'd rather be out there herding cattle, sleeping on the range. My head's clearer out there. To be honest, even that hasn't made me feel like I belong here lately."

"I think I know how you feel. I mean, I thought opening the store and being successful would make me happy. And it did in a lot of ways. I'm still proud of myself for pushing through all those hard times, those early-morning shifts at the coffee house and late nights doing paperwork for the shop. I still love finding an amazing artist and helping them make a living from their art. That's the part that feels good about what I do," she said. "But all of my success didn't make *me* happy. Having money—don't get me wrong I'm nowhere near your family's level of success—wasn't as fulfilling as I thought it would be."

"You could've asked me outright and I'd have told you that much," he teased.

"Lotta good it does me right now," she replied, appreciating a break from the sadness that threatened to overwhelm her, to suck her under. "Let me know when you unlock all of life's mysteries, will you?"

"You'll be my first call," he said, then added, "Look at you, though. You're successful. Beautiful inside and out. I'm proud of you, Kelly. I always have been."

"We've come a long way since fifth grade. Haven't we?" she asked, but inside her mind went down a different path. Proud of what? The fact that she'd let down her cousin in the worst possible way? Why was taking a compliment so hard? Her mother's last words to Kelly wound through her thoughts. *If you can find a man who'll take you and you get married try not to mess it up.* Kelly had been waiting for the words *like I did.* But they never came. Why did her mother's words have a way of winding back through her thoughts at times like these? Why did she let those old memories control her thoughts? Cause her to rein in her emotions the minute she felt them going down the path of love?

A little voice in the back of Kelly's mind said, *if your own mother can't love you, then who can?*

The break didn't last for long as thoughts of her cousin came flooding back. Christina had been mother and father, friend and relative. She couldn't let Christina down.

Kelly was more determined than ever to seek justice for her cousin. True justice. The men in jail might've been the lackeys but she knew down deep they hadn't orchestrated this and she'd bet money the Hardaways were involved. Proving it was another story. Finding proof would lead her down the same path as her cousin.

She rolled away from Will and sat up, scooting toward the edge of the bed. "Are you hungry? I'll get something to eat from the fridge."

Meals had been prepared and were ready to heat and eat. For someone who had as much money as Will, he never made anyone else around him feel less because of it. He'd always been down-to-earth and that was another thing she loved about him.

Loved?

Talk about putting the cart before the horse. But then, she'd known him since they were twelve years old.

They had so much history and friendship.

So, yeah, she loved him.

"Let me get up and help," he said, wincing as he forced himself to sitting position. He'd pushed his body too far during sex.

Guilt impaled her. "Stay here. I know my way to the kitchen."

"That may be but no one makes better coffee than I do," he quipped, bending forward and taking in a sharp breath as he stood. He was masking how much effort it was taking to stand on his own two feet.

"Your coffeemaker takes pods." Fist to hip, she called him out.

"Yeah, but I know just the right amount of water to pour," he said.

Kelly smiled despite herself.

With everything going on she didn't want to laugh. She didn't want to disrespect her cousin in that way. And that was probably silly to think that she had to suffer in order for Christina to be happy.

Christina, of all people, would want Kelly to experience joy.

It was Kelly who couldn't let herself.

THREE MORE DAYS passed. Will was getting stronger. Kelly felt more and more content being with him at the ranch.

People seemed to be returning to normal routines.

Kelly couldn't afford to get comfortable.

This had been a fantastic place to heal and recharge. Her body still ached in places but her cuts, scrapes and bruises were much better. Christmas was coming in a few days and she'd been away from work too long.

"I think it's time for me to visit my store," she finally said over breakfast of muffins and coffee. Before Will could argue, she added, "I've been gone for two weeks without making contact with my employees. They need to see me and I need to see them. This is our busy season. Your cousin said it would be unlikely for Hardaway or his family to make a move on me considering how much their activities are being monitored. Even they wouldn't be bold enough to get caught. The men doing their bidding haven't recanted their stories no matter how many angles Zach has come at them from."

Will set down his mug. "I'll drive."

"Are you sure that's a good idea?"

"I'm fine."

"I wasn't talking about your injuries," she said.

He pinned her with his stare. "What's that supposed to mean?"

"I'm just saying. You used to play poker. Right? Isn't it time to fold a losing hand," she said. Those words were difficult to say but someone had to point to reason.

"You're not a losing hand, Kelly." His voice was irritated as he walked over to her and brushed a kiss on her lips.

She loved the way he tasted.

"Believe me, I know what it's like to look for the door in pretty much every relationship I've been involved with. Hell, the last one only moved forward because I'd been given an ultimatum. Get hitched or go. Even though we almost went through with the ceremony and it still hurt like hell to be left at the altar, I'm grateful Lacey walked. She did us both a favor. I didn't see it that way at first but I do now," he said.

"I care about you, Will. I do. But I'm not in a good place to think about anything serious developing between us if that's what you're saying." She hated the way her words seemed like a physical blow.

"Give me a heads-up when you plan to pack up. Will you?" It was all he said before he walked out of the kitchen.

She wanted to run after him and tell him that she was sorry. That she loved him and losing him would crush her.

Why couldn't she let go of the past and let herself be happy?

Chapter Twenty-One

The store looked fine from the outside. Her apartment building had suffered enough damage to displace roughly fifty out of two hundred residents.

Sydney had opened the store ten minutes ago when Will parked after circling the block three times to be safe.

The ride to the store had been quiet—too quiet. The easy way Kelly had with Will had felt pinched off. Granted, she got it. She understood that she'd pushed him away. A gorgeous man like Will didn't have to wait around for anyone until she was ready. And Kelly might never be ready to take that step with anyone, to let someone in where she was vulnerable and could be crushed.

The minute Kelly walked inside, Sydney rushed her. Her employee, a petite brunette in her mid-twenties, was a student at nearby UNT's Fort Worth campus.

"It's so good to see you," Sydney said as she wrapped her arms around Kelly, but her gaze was on the man standing a couple of steps behind.

Kelly embraced Sydney and then introduced her to Will.

Sydney blushed.

Since hiring her there'd been a number of male customers coming in, looking for gift pieces for their moms or sisters. Kelly knew it was because they wanted to have a reason to speak to Sydney outside of the classroom. Never had there been more UNT T-shirt-wearing guys buying jewelry. She saw their infatuation with Sydney in their eyes.

The fact that Sydney's face flushed as she talked to Will sent a jolt of jealousy Kelly had no right to own shooting through her.

"How's the store been?" Kelly steered her thoughts back on track.

"Good. Sales have been strong," Sydney reported. "I saw the fire and I freaked."

"I'm sorry that I couldn't make contact right away," Kelly stated. "You got my note, though, right?"

"What note?" Sydney's eyebrows pinched together over bright brown eyes.

Kelly walked around, looking at the tile floor for a corner of paper sticking out. There were several glass cases so customers could roam around.

"I slipped one under the door a couple of days ago to let you guys know I was okay and to keep things running until I return," she said. A little more than two weeks had passed since Will was in the hospital. Christmas might be days away and decorations might be everywhere she looked but Kelly couldn't rally a holiday spirit and especially while making funeral plans for Christina.

Sydney shrugged and stared blankly, quickly joining her boss in the search. "We got together and figured out how to cover shifts when we didn't hear from you."

"It has to be here somewhere." Kelly dropped down on all fours near the door.

Will was already on all fours, scouring the floor for signs of the note.

"I wonder if someone threw it away by accident." Sydney checked underneath a case. "Hold on a minute."

Kelly was next to her in two seconds flat.

Sydney held up two pieces of paper.

"There should only be one." Kelly glanced up at Will, who stood with great effort. And then she took the offering.

Kelly recognized her note. It had been scratched out on legal-pad paper from Will's vehicle and folded twice.

The other looked like white printer paper.

She held it in her hand as Will helped her to her feet. She opened it and smoothed out the rough edges on the nearest counter.

I got proof. Those were the first three words on a handwritten note from Christina.

> Hardaway's father contracted Bobby Flynn to make your dad disappear before he could rat them out on a real estate deal. They used your

pop's social security number on a deal for the land in Snyder, Texas, so it couldn't be traced back to them. He got a payout, but when he figured out what the deal was worth he went back to them for more money. Bobby's serving time in Huntsville, where I've been going. Said he's got nothing to lose by talking to me since he's in for life on an unrelated charge and never got to enjoy the money the Hardaways had promised. He ended up going to jail for a break-in that went bad and somehow he's sure they're behind him getting life.

Bobby said he can prove he committed the crime. And he's real sorry about your brother. What a jackass—Bobby that is. He said that his job was to make it look like an accident.

Anyway, I'm real sorry.

A few guys have been following me and I had to hide this somewhere I knew you'd find it. Even if it was during the holiday rush.

Love ya, girl!

Kelly wiped away the stray tears that had fallen. She looked at Will. "Let's call Zach."

"That note is evidence, so we'll leave it right here until he comes for it." Will took a picture of the note and immediately texted it to Zach.

Kelly understood what he was saying. Courts would want to prove that was Christina's handwriting and also that she'd been the one to deliver it.

Kelly's fingerprints were already on it, as were Sydney's. No one else could touch it.

There was proof. Hardaway and his family would be arrested and brought to justice.

"Can you get Zach on the line?" she asked.

Will nodded.

He put the phone on speaker and brought Zach up to speed.

"I'll call Fort Worth P.D. and have them send an officer to pick up the evidence," Zach said. "The three men who are under arrest work for Hardaway's company as security."

"Is there any way I can be notified when the Hardaways are brought in? I'd like to see it with my own eyes," Kelly asked.

"I'll be sure to alert you," Zach promised.

"Is there any chance they can skirt these charges? I mean, they'll go to jail for this, right?" she asked.

"They'll have solid attorneys who know how to bend the law," he admitted. "But the DA is no slouch. The evidence is strong. I'm confident they'll do their time."

Those words brought so much relief, which washed over Kelly.

"Thank you," she said to Zach before ending the call. She turned to Will. "I didn't think about this before but if I'd married Fletcher his family would gain access to the land outright."

"In Texas they wouldn't be able to take it from you. Anything you owned before the marriage would've been yours," Will stated.

"I'm pretty sure that I wouldn't have made it home after the wedding. If the pastor hadn't delayed the wedding I would've been dead soon after. I'm sure of it," she said on a sigh. "My apartment building isn't going to reopen for a few weeks. Any chance I can stay with you until then?"

"You can stay with me as long as you want, Kelly. You know I'll always be there for you."

She walked to him and pressed up to her tiptoes. Her hands on his chest, she kissed him, loving the taste of coffee still on his tongue.

"Be careful or I might just believe you."

THE DA HAD TAKEN less than twenty-four hours to fact-check and build a case against the Hardaways. Will knew that Kelly had been on edge waiting for the call to come that the arrest was going down.

It came at eight o'clock that Friday night.

Zach had phoned to let them know that Fletcher's father was responsible for the deaths of Kelly's father and brother. However, Fletcher alone was responsible for Christina's murder.

With the evidence that had been collected—everything Christina had said turned out to be true and verifiable—the two were going to spend the rest of their lives behind bars.

The drive to Tarrant County jail was solemn.

There was no media present, as Will had feared there might be.

Kelly exited his vehicle and he linked their fingers together as they walked toward the building.

"Did Zach say where we'd get the best view?" she asked.

"How close do you want to be?"

"I don't have anything to say to either one of them. Nothing would bring my family back, anyway. I just want to see them walking up those stairs in handcuffs." Her serious eyes focused on the pavement. He could feel her hand shaking in his so he stopped her.

She looked up at him and he dipped down and captured her lips.

She kissed him back, wrapping her arms around his neck.

When they broke free, he rested his forehead against hers.

"You don't have to do this if you don't want to," he said, a little out of breath from the intensity of the kiss.

"Believe it or not, I'll be okay," she said. "I know I've been quiet lately and I'm not always so good at talking about what's going on inside my head. I also know that I've said hurtful things to push you away and I'm truly sorry for that. I can look at these men because they represent my past and I'm ready to put that behind me. I'll never stop missing my family and it'll never be okay that they're gone." She paused long enough to bite her bottom lip. "But when I look into the future, you're the only person I see, Will. I'm scared of that, of getting hurt if you decide I'm not enough someday. But I love you with all my heart. And I think I have since fifth grade."

Will brought his hand to her face to touch her. He looked into her eyes and found home.

"There'll never come a time when I don't need you, Kelly. I'm hooked. The ranch never truly felt like my home until you arrived. We can build a life together there." He took a knee as tears spilled from her eyes. Happy tears this time. "I'm proposing marriage because I love you with all my heart. You don't have to give me an answer right now. I'll wait for you until you're ready. But I want you to know I'm all in and that's never going to change."

Kelly's smile lit up the night.

"That's a good thing, Will. Because I'm not letting you go this time."

He stood and captured her face in his hands.

"I love you," he said again with his lips pressed to hers.

A cruiser pulled up with another on its tail.

Will laced his and Kelly's fingers together as she turned around to face the building.

An officer stepped out of the driver's side as several officers came out of the building, rushing down the stairs.

The second cruiser parked behind the first and waited.

First, the senior Hardaway was led out of the back of an SUV and walked into the side door of the jail as Kelly got to watch justice for Christina play out. Next, Fletcher stepped out of a vehicle, looking pale and like he might throw up. No doubt, his family would hire lawyers. But Zach had reassured Will that the evidence would hold.

"He's going down for his crimes and for obstruction of justice for interfering with a murder investigation by offering a reward." Will stood beside her as she leaned into him.

Kelly tugged at his hand. After the holidays, she said she planned to have a small ceremony for Christina. He'd offer whatever support she needed.

"Can we go home now?" And then she added, "For keeps this time."

The thought of taking Kelly home for good was enough high-stakes excitement for Will. He no longer felt like he needed to prove something to the world, or chase the next adrenaline rush. Being with Kelly on the land he loved would be enough—she was enough.

"Let's go home."

* * * * *

Look for the next book in USA TODAY *bestselling author Barb Han's Rushing Creek Crime Spree miniseries,* Ambushed at Christmas, *available next month*

And don't miss the previous title in the series:

Cornered at Christmas

Available now from Harlequin Intrigue!

COMING NEXT MONTH FROM

HARLEQUIN®

INTRIGUE

Available November 19, 2019

#1893 SAFETY BREACH

Longview Ridge Ranch • by Delores Fossen

Former profiler Gemma Hanson is in witness protection, but she's still haunted by memories of the serial killer who tried to kill her last year. Her concerns skyrocket when Sheriff Kellan Slater tells her the murderer has learned her location and is coming to finish what he started.

#1894 UNDERCOVER ACCOMPLICE

Red, White and Built: Delta Force Deliverance

by Carol Ericson

When Delta Force soldier Hunter Mancini learns the group that kidnapped CIA operative Sue Chandler is now framing his team leader, he asks for her help. But could she be hiding something that would clear his boss?

#1895 AMBUSHED AT CHRISTMAS

Rushing Creek Crime Spree • by Barb Han

After a jogger resembling Detective Leah Cordon is murdered, rancher Deacon Kent approaches her, believing the attack is related to recent cattle mutilations. Can they find the killer before he corners Leah?

#1896 DANGEROUS CONDITIONS

Protectors at Heart • by Jenna Kernan

Former soldier Logan Lynch's first investigation as the constable of a small town leads him to microbiologist Paige Morris, whose boss was killed. Yet as they search for the murderer, Paige is forced to reveal a secret that shows the stakes couldn't be higher.

#1897 RULES IN DEFIANCE

Blackhawk Security • by Nichole Severn

Blackhawk Security investigator Elliot Dunham never expected his neighbor to show up bruised and covered in blood in the middle of the night. To protect Waylynn Hargraves, Elliot must defy the rules he's set for himself, because he knows he's all that stands between her and certain death.

#1898 HIDDEN TRUTH

Stealth • by Danica Winters

When undercover CIA agent Trevor Martin meets Sabrina Parker, the housekeeper at the ranch where he's lying low, he doesn't know she's an undercover FBI agent. After a murder on the property, the operatives must work together, but can they discover their hidden connection before it's too late?

YOU CAN FIND MORE INFORMATION ON UPCOMING HARLEQUIN® TITLES, FREE EXCERPTS AND MORE AT WWW.HARLEQUIN.COM.

HICNM1119

Get 4 FREE REWARDS!

We'll send you 2 FREE Books <u>plus</u> 2 FREE Mystery Gifts.

Harlequin Intrigue® books feature heroes and heroines that confront and survive danger while finding themselves irresistibly drawn to one another.

YES! Please send me 2 FREE Harlequin Intrigue® novels and my 2 FREE gifts (gifts are worth about $10 retail). After receiving them, if I don't wish to receive any more books, I can return the shipping statement marked "cancel." If I don't cancel, I will receive 6 brand-new novels every month and be billed just $4.99 each for the regular-print edition or $5.99 each for the larger-print edition in the U.S., or $5.74 each for the regular-print edition or $6.49 each for the larger-print edition in Canada. That's a savings of at least 12% off the cover price! It's quite a bargain! Shipping and handling is just 50¢ per book in the U.S. and $1.25 per book in Canada.* I understand that accepting the 2 free books and gifts places me under no obligation to buy anything. I can always return a shipment and cancel at any time. The free books and gifts are mine to keep no matter what I decide.

Choose one: ☐ **Harlequin Intrigue® Regular-Print** (182/382 HDN GNXC) ☐ **Harlequin Intrigue® Larger-Print** (199/399 HDN GNXC)

Name (please print)

Address Apt. #

City State/Province Zip/Postal Code

Mail to the **Reader Service:**
IN U.S.A.: P.O. Box 1341, Buffalo, NY 14240-8531
IN CANADA: P.O. Box 603, Fort Erie, Ontario L2A 5X3

Want to try 2 free books from another series? Call 1-800-873-8635 or visit www.ReaderService.com.

*Terms and prices subject to change without notice. Prices do not include sales taxes, which will be charged (if applicable) based on your state or country of residence. Canadian residents will be charged applicable taxes. Offer not valid in Quebec. This offer is limited to one order per household. Books received may not be as shown. Not valid for current subscribers to Harlequin Intrigue books. All orders subject to approval. Credit or debit balances in a customer's account(s) may be offset by any other outstanding balance owed by or to the customer. Please allow 4 to 6 weeks for delivery. Offer available while quantities last.

Your Privacy—The Reader Service is committed to protecting your privacy. Our Privacy Policy is available online at www.ReaderService.com or upon request from the Reader Service. We make a portion of our mailing list available to reputable third parties that offer products we believe may interest you. If you prefer that we not exchange your name with third parties, or if you wish to clarify or modify your communication preferences, please visit us at www.ReaderService.com/consumerschoice or write to us at Reader Service Preference Service, P.O. Box 9062, Buffalo, NY 14240-9062. Include your complete name and address.

HI20

SPECIAL EXCERPT FROM

HARLEQUIN®

INTRIGUE

When her WITSEC location is compromised, former profiler Gemma Hanson turns to the only man who can keep her safe: Sheriff Kellan Slater. The only problem is, they share a complicated past...and an intense chemistry that has never cooled.

Read on for a sneak peek of Safety Breach, *part of Longview Ridge Ranch by* USA TODAY *bestselling author Delores Fossen.*

"Why did you say you owed me?" she asked.

The question came out of the blue and threw him, so much so that he gulped down too much coffee and nearly choked. Hardly the reaction for a tough-nosed cop. But his reaction to her hadn't exactly been all badge, either.

Kellan lifted his shoulder and wanted to kick himself for ever bringing it up in the first place. Bad timing, he thought, and wondered if there would ever be a good time for him to grovel.

"I didn't stop Eric from shooting you that night." He said that fast. Not a drop of sugarcoating. "You, my father and Dusty. I'm sorry for that."

Her silence and the shimmering look in her eyes made him stupid, and that was the only excuse he could come up with for why he kept talking.

HSEEXP50496

"It's easier for me to toss some of the blame at you for not ID'ing a killer sooner," he added. And he still did blame her, in part, for that. "But it was my job to stop him before he killed two people and injured another while he was right under my nose."

The silence just kept on going. So much so that Kellan turned, ready to go back to his desk so that he wouldn't continue to prattle on. Gemma stopped him by putting her hand on his arm. It was like a trigger that sent his gaze searching for hers. Wasn't hard to find when she stood and met him eye to eye.

"It was easier for me to toss some of the blame at you, too." She made another of those sighs. "But there was no stopping Eric that night. The stopping should have happened prior to that. I should have seen the signs." When he started to speak, Gemma lifted her hand to silence him. "And please don't tell me that it's all right, that I'm not at fault. I don't think I could take that right now."

Unfortunately, Kellan understood just what she meant. They were both still hurting, and a mutual sympathyfest was only going to make it harder. They couldn't go back. Couldn't undo. And that left them with only one direction. Looking ahead and putting this son of a bitch in a hole where he belonged.

Don't miss Safety Breach *by Delores Fossen,*
available December 2019 wherever
Harlequin® Intrigue books and ebooks are sold.

Harlequin.com

Copyright © 2019 by Delores Fossen

HSEEXP50496

Don't miss this holiday Western romance from *USA TODAY* bestselling author

DELORES FOSSEN

Sometimes a little Christmas magic can rekindle the most unexpected romances...

"Fossen creates sexy cowboys and fast-moving plots that will take your breath away." —Lori Wilde, *New York Times* bestselling author

Order your copy today!

HQNBooks.com

PHDFCWC1119

Need an adrenaline rush from nail-biting tales
(and irresistible males)?

Check out **Harlequin Intrigue®**
and **Harlequin® Romantic Suspense** books!

New books available every month!

CONNECT WITH US AT:

Facebook.com/groups/HarlequinConnection

Facebook.com/HarlequinBooks

Twitter.com/HarlequinBooks

Instagram.com/HarlequinBooks

Pinterest.com/HarlequinBooks

ReaderService.com

**ROMANCE WHEN
YOU NEED IT**

SGENRE2018